"Have fun Penny," Carter drawled softly as they hit the pavement.

She turned and fluttered him a look that was one eyelash short of do-me-now. "Oh, I plan to."

So she couldn't resist the sparks, either. And he so knew the type of fun girls like her enjoyed—the eat-men-for-breakfast kind. He smiled, happy to play if she wanted, because experience had made him too tough to chew. She could learn that if she dared.

Testosterone—and other things—surged again. So did his latent combative nature. That vulnerability he'd seen upstairs when he'd startled her, and again after he'd kissed her? A mirage—she'd been buying time while assessing her position. She'd want to bring Carter to heel like every other man she knew. Yeah, he'd seen her vixen desire for dominance. She thought she could toy with him like some feline would a mouse.

She was so wrong.

But he could hardly wait for her to bring it on.

Possibly the only librarian who got told off herself for talking too much, **NATALIE ANDERSON** decided writing books might be more fun than shelving them—and, boy, is it that! Especially writing romance—it's the realization of a lifetime dream kick-started by many an afternoon spent devouring Grandma's Harlequin romance novels.

She lives in New Zealand, with her husband and four gorgeous-but-exhausting children. Swing by her website anytime—she'd love to hear from you: www.natalie-anderson.com.

THE END OF FAKING IT
NATALIE ANDERSON

~ His Very Personal Assistant ~

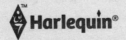

TORONTO NEW YORK LONDON
AMSTERDAM PARIS SYDNEY HAMBURG
STOCKHOLM ATHENS TOKYO MILAN MADRID
PRAGUE WARSAW BUDAPEST AUCKLAND

Recycling programs
for this product may
not exist in your area.

ISBN-13: 978-0-373-52823-3

THE END OF FAKING IT

First North American Publication 2011

Copyright © 2011 by Natalie Anderson

www.Harlequin.com

Printed in U.S.A.

THE END OF FAKING IT

For my awesome daily support structure:
Dave, Mum & Soraya.

You guys helped with the heartache of
this one especially.

Am so happy to be returning the favour now,
Soraya!

CHAPTER ONE

ANOTHER two minutes couldn't possibly matter—late was late and this was too important to leave.

'Come on, Audrey,' Penny muttered softly. 'Let's keep you all healthy, huh?' She scattered the plant food and put the pack back in the top drawer of the filing cabinet. Then she picked up the jug of water.

'What are you doing?'

Her fingers flinched and she whirled at the sound of deep, accusing anger. She saw black clothes, big frame, even bigger frown. Striding towards her was a total stranger. A tall, dark, two hundred per cent testosterone-filled male was in her office, late at night. Not Jed the security guard, but a hard edged predator coming straight for her—fast.

She flung forward, all raw reflex.

He swore as water hit him straight in the eyes. She lunged again, hoping to knock him out with a Pyrex jug to the temple. Only halfway there her arm slammed against something hard, whiplash sent shudders down her shoulder. Painfully strong fingers held her wrist vice-tight. She immediately strained to break free, twisting skin and muscle. He sharply wrenched her wrist. She gasped. Her fingers failed and the jug tipped between them.

The shock of the ice-cold water splashing across her chest suffocated her shriek. She recoiled, but he came forward relentlessly, still death-gripping her wrist. The drawer slammed as she backed up and banged against it.

'Who the hell are you and what are you doing in here?' he demanded, storming further into her personal space.

Shock, pain, fear. She couldn't move other than to blink, trying to see clearly and figure a way to escape.

But he moved closer still. 'What are you doing with the files?' Pure menace.

The cold metal cabinet dug into her back. But he wasn't in the least cold. She could feel his heat even with the slight distance between them. His hand branded her. Her scream couldn't emerge—not with her throat squeezed so tight and her heart not beating at all.

He pushed back his fringe with his free hand, also blinked several times—only his eyes were filled with the water she'd thrown at him, not tears like hers. He actually laughed—not nicely—and his grip tightened even more. 'I didn't think this was going to be that easy.' He looked over her, scorn sharpening every harsh word. 'You're not screwing another cent out of this company.'

Penny gaped. He was insane. Totally insane. 'The security guard will be doing his rounds any minute,' she panted. 'He's armed.'

'With what—chewing gum? The only person going to the police cells tonight is you, honey.'

Yep, totally insane. Unfortunately he was also right about Jed's lack of ammo—the best she could hope for was a heavy torch. And it was a hopeless hope because she'd been lying anyway—Jed didn't do rounds. He sat at his desk. And she was ten floors up, alone with a complete nut-job who was going to…going to…

Jerky breathing filled her ears—as if someone was having an asthma attack. It took long moments to realise it was her. She pressed her free hand to her stomach, but couldn't stop the violent tremors. Her eyes watered more, her muscles quivered. Dimly she heard him swear.

'I'm not going to hurt you,' he said loudly right in her face.

'You already are,' she squeaked.

He instantly let go of her wrist, but he didn't move away. If anything he towered closer, still blocking her exit. But she could breathe again and her brain started sending signals. Then her heart got going, pushing a plan along her veins. All she had to do was escape him somehow and race down to Jed on Reception. She could do that, right? She forced a few more deep breaths as both fight and flight instincts rose and merged, locking her body and brain into survive mode.

'Who are you and what are you doing here?' he asked, a little quieter that time, but still with that peremptory tone, as if he had all the authority.

Which he didn't.

'Answer that yourself,' Penny snapped back.

He glanced down to where the jug lay useless on the floor and, beside her, where the plant's tub sat. 'You're the cleaner?' He looked from her toes back up to her face—slowly. 'You don't look like a cleaner.'

'No, who are *you* and what are *you* doing here?' Now she could see—and almost think—she took stock of him. Tall and dark, yes, but while the jeans and tee were black, they were well fitting—as in designer fitting. And it wasn't as if he was wearing a balaclava. Not exactly hardcore crim kind of clothing. The intensely angry look had vanished, and his face was open and sun-burnished, as if he spent time skiing or sailing. The hard planes of his body, and the strength she felt firsthand, suggested a high degree of fitness too. On his wrist was one of those impressive watches, all masculine and metal with a million little dials and functions most people wouldn't be able to figure out. And now that the water was gone from her eyes she could see his were an amazing blue-green. Clear and shining and vibrant and…were they checking her out?

'I asked you first,' he said softly, putting his hands either side of her to rest on the top of the filing cabinet. His arms made long, strong, bronzed prison bars.

'I'm the PA,' she answered mechanically, most of her attention focused on digesting this new element of his proximity. 'This is my desk.'

'*You're* Penny?' His brows skyrocketed up and he blatantly checked over her outfit again. 'You definitely don't look like any PA Mason would have.'

How did he know her name? And Mason? Her eyes narrowed as the gleam in his grew. Heat radiated out from him, warming her blood and making her skin super-sensitive. No way. She wasn't going to let him look at her like *that*. She sucked up some sarcasm. 'Actually Mason really likes my skirt.'

He angled his head and studied it yet again. 'Is that what that is? I thought it was a belt.' He smiled. Not a scary psycho-killer smile, more one that would make a million hearts flutter and two million legs start to slide apart—like hers suddenly threatened to.

It was that powerful she had to consciously order her

lips not to smile right back at him like some besotted bimbo. 'It's vintage Levi's.'

'Oh, that explains it. You didn't realise moths had been at the hem?' His face lit up even more. 'Not that I'm complaining.'

Okay, the denim mini was teensy weensy, the heels of her shoes super-high and her curve-clinging champagne-coloured blouse off the shoulder. Of course she didn't wear this to work. She was all dressed up for dance-party pleasure. Yes, she'd dressed in case there was that other sort of pleasure to be had as well—just because she hadn't found a playmate in a while, didn't mean she'd given up all hope. Only now the pretty silk was sopping, plastered to her chest, revealing far more than she'd ever intended. And she was not, *not*, feeling any kind of primal response to a random stranger who'd all but assaulted her. 'Before I scream, who are you?' Not that there was any need to scream now and she knew it.

'I work here,' he said smoothly.

'I know everyone who works in this building and you don't.'

He reached into his pocket and then dangled a security card in her face. She quickly read the name—Carter Dodds. It didn't enlighten her in the least; she'd never heard of him. Then she looked at the photo. In it he was wearing the black tee shirt that he had on now.

Amazingly her brain managed the simple computation. 'You started today.'

'Officially tomorrow.' He nodded.

'Then why are you here now?' And how? Jed might be slack on the rounds but he was scrupulous about knowing who was still in the building after hours. And surely

Mason wouldn't have let a new recruit have open access to everything with no one around to supervise?

'I wanted to see what the place was like when it was quiet.'

'Why?' Her suspicions grew more. What did he want to see? There wasn't any money kept on site, but there were files, transactions, account numbers—loads of sensitive investor information worth millions. She glanced past him to Mason's open office door, but could hear no gentle hum of the computer.

'Why are you watering the plants at nine-thirty at night?' he countered.

'I forgot to do it earlier.'

'So you came back specially?' Utter disbelief.

Actually she'd been downstairs swimming in the pool—breaking all the rules because it was after the gym's closing hour. But she wasn't going to drop Jed in it. 'New recruits don't get to grill me.'

'No?'

His smile sharpened, but before he could get another question out she got in one of hers. 'How come you're here alone?'

'Mason wanted to get an early night before we get started tomorrow.'

'He didn't tell me you were starting.'

'Does he tell you everything?'

'Usually.' She lifted her chin in defiance of the calculated look that crossed his face, but he missed it—his focus had dropped to her body again.

'Mason buried his heart with his wife,' he said bluntly. 'You won't get any gold out of him no matter how short your skirt.'

Her mouth fell open. *'What?'*

'You wouldn't be the first pretty girl to bat her eye-lashes at a rich old man.'

What was he suggesting? 'Mason's *eighty*.'

His shrug didn't hide his anger. 'For some women that would make him all the more attractive.'

'Yeah, well, not me. He's like my grandfather.' She screwed up her face.

'You're the one who said he likes your skirt.'

'Only because you couldn't drag your eyes from it.'

'But isn't that why you wear it?'

She paused. He wasn't afraid to challenge direct, was he? Well, nor was she—when she could think. Right now her brain had gone all lame. 'I don't believe you're supposed to be here now.'

'Really? Go ahead and ask your boss. Use my phone.' He pulled it out of his pocket, pressed buttons and handed it to her.

It rang only a couple of times.

'Carter, have you already found something?'

Penny gripped the phone tighter as she absorbed the anxiety in Mason's quick-fire query. 'No, sorry, Mason, it's Penny. Not Carter.' She stuttered when she saw Carter's sudden grin—disarming and devilish. 'Look, I've just bumped into someone in the office.'

'Carter,' Mason said.

'Yes.' Penny winced at the obvious. Had the sinking feeling she was about to wince even more. 'He's given me his phone to call you.'

'Penny, I'm sorry, I should have told you but Carter thought it should wait until he got there.'

Thought what should wait? Why was Carter the one calling shots? What was going on?

'Carter heads up Dodds WD in Melbourne. I asked

him to come to Sydney for a couple of weeks. I need his help.'

'What for?'

Carter knew he was still standing too close but too bad. In fact he put both hands back on either side of her. That way she couldn't readily escape. He was certain she would, so he made sure she couldn't—by holding a position that was only a few inches away from intimate.

He was having a time shutting up the temptation whispering that he should lose those few inches. He pushed his hands hard on the cool metal and watched as she pressed the phone closer to her ear and turned her head away from him.

The colour ran under her skin like an incoming tide and Carter couldn't contain his amusement. Mason was his grandfather's best friend. He'd seen him every few months all his life and he was on the old boy's speed-dial to prove it. This was the first time Mason had asked him for help—and help he would. But just this moment?

Distraction. Capital D.

'Of course.' Penny had turned her head even further away, clearly hoping he wouldn't hear whatever it was that Mason was saying.

Carter didn't give a damn what the old guy said right now. He was too lost in looking at her. She had the biggest, darkest eyes he'd ever seen. They drew him in and sucked him under—like sparkling pools that turned out to be dangerously deep, the kind of eyes that you could stare into endlessly—and he was. Peripherally, bits of his body were absorbing the detail of hers and the back of his brain drew rapid conclusions.

A skirt that short, a shirt that sexy, a body that honed, lips that slicked...

This woman knew how attractive she was, and she emphasised all her best assets. Everything about her was polished to pure, sensual perfection. She was no shy, shrinking secretary. She was a siren. And every basic cell in Carter's body wanted to answer her summons. So, so badly.

'Hello?'

She was holding the phone out to him and he'd been too busy gawping to notice. He grabbed it and started talking.

'Hi, Mason, sorry to bother you so late.'

'It doesn't matter. It's great you're onto it so quickly. I can't thank you enough.'

'So Penny's your temp PA?' Carter kept looking at her, still struggling to believe that conservative, eighty-year-old Mason had ever hired such a blatant sex bomb. 'She's working late.'

'She always works late.' Mason sounded pleased. 'She's an angel. I get in every morning and everything is so organised, she makes it a breeze.'

An *angel*? Carter's suspicions sharpened again. Penny wouldn't be the first attractive young woman to turn an older man's head. Carter knew exactly how easy it was for an avaricious, ambitious female to use her beauty to dazzle a fool old enough to know better. He'd watched not one, but two do that to his dad. Despite her outraged reaction, who was to say that wasn't what was happening here? 'How long has she been with you?' He couldn't not ask.

There was a silence. 'Since after the problem started.'

Mason's voice turned arctic. 'I thought I'd made this clear already.'

Yeah. Mason had mentioned his fabulous PA more than once—but not her hotter-than-Venus factor. Not mentioning that didn't seem natural.

'You tell her what's going on,' Mason said sharply. 'I should have already. Carter, she's not who you're looking for.'

Carter stared at the temptation personified before him. Her mouth was as glossy and red ripe as a Morello cherry—and he wanted a taste. That was the real problem. Hell, he was off on a tangent before he'd even started. He owed Mason better than this. 'You're right,' he said brusquely. 'She's not.'

Penny watched him pocket the phone. He didn't seem to be any happier about the situation—offered no laughter or light apology. If anything he looked as angry as he had when he'd first interrogated her. What was he here to do exactly? Mason hadn't elaborated, just told her to help him if he asked her to. They hadn't advertised a new job—she was the one who placed the ads so she'd know. So this was cronyism, some old boys' school network thing. But he was hardly a fresh-faced graduate getting his first contract courtesy of his father. 'You know Mason personally,' she said baldly, annoyed by the fact—annoyed by him—and his attractiveness.

'Have done for years.' He nodded.

Yeah, that was why the job, whatever it was, hadn't been advertised. Mason had probably made something up for him to do. Still smarting from his gold-digger slur, she let her inner bitch out to taunt. 'You don't look like you have to pull favours to get a job.'

'Don't I?' he answered too softly. 'How would you know? Is that what you do?' He leaned closer and whispered low, as if they were intimate. 'What kind of favours do you pull to score a job, Penny?'

Okay, she'd crossed the line a little, but he'd just leapt it. 'What sort of favours do you think I *pull*?' she fired back before thinking.

His eyes flashed, the pupils expanding so fast the piercing colours became the thinnest of circles around the burgeoning black. Riveted, she watched the myriad greens and blues narrow out. He really did have it—perfect symmetry, angular jawbones and hair that just begged to be ruffled and then gripped tight.

The palms of her hands tingled, heated. Only it wasn't just his hair she imagined pulling close, no, now she was pulling on hot, silky hard skin, stroking it faster and faster and—*OMG where had that come from?*

She gulped back the insanity. She couldn't be thinking that. She looked down and clamped her mouth shut, swallowing both literally and mentally, overly aware her breathing had quickened to audible—basically to panting. Again.

Oh, please don't let him know what she'd been thinking. She glanced back up at him. All the blue had gone from his irises leaving nothing but thin rings of green fire around those huge, black pupils. Dusky red tinged his cheekbones. She could relate. Blood was firing all round her body, pinking up all sorts of parts—her face included. But at least he wasn't panting like some dog in heat, which she, unfortunately, was.

He said nothing, she said nothing. But she could see it shimmering in the air between them—razor-sharp attraction. Urges at their most basic. Urges almost uncontrollable.

'There's a problem in the accounts—someone in the company is skimming,' he suddenly said roughly, jerking his head up.

'What?'

'I'm here to check through all the files and find out who and how.'

Someone was stealing? And Carter was here to catch him? Mason had said he headed up some company in Melbourne, so was he some kind of CEO/forensic accountant or something?

Actually that didn't seem to fit. Not when he wore jeans and tousled hair so well. He looked as if he had too much street cred to be a number cruncher.

'The only people who'll know the real reason I'm here are you, Mason and me,' he continued. 'We'll spread it 'round the company that I'm a friend of Mason's who's borrowing an office for a couple of weeks. Which I am.'

The fiery green in his eyes dampened to cold blue serious. The sensual curve of his mouth flattened to a straight, hard line. Penny stared, watching him ice over, as she absorbed that info and the implications.

Then she realised. 'You thought it was *me*?' She basically shrieked, her temperature steaming back up to boiling point. She might be many things, but a thief wasn't one of them. 'I'm the best damn temp in this town. I'm hardworking and honest. How dare you storm in here and throw round your gutter accusations?'

'I know.' His expression went very intense. 'I'm sorry. Mason already told me it couldn't be you.'

He sucked the wind right out of her sails and disarmed

her completely with a sudden flash of that smile. It cracked his icy cover and let the heat ripple once more. But she refused to let her anger slide into attraction. 'You still thought it,' she accused.

'Well, you have to admit it looked…it looked…' His attention wandered—down. 'It looked…'

Her body—despite the freezing wet shirt—was burning. Okay, that attraction was impossible to stop—simplest thing now would be to escape. 'Well, now that you've done your looking,' she said sarcastically, her eyes locked on his, 'are you going to step back and let me past?'

'Not yet,' he said wryly. 'I'm still looking.'

Penny's nerves tightened to one notch the other side of screaming. His lashes lowered and his smile faded. She looked down too. Now her silk shirt was wet it was both skin colour and skin tight and she might as well not be wearing anything. Even worse, she was aching…and horrified to realise it was completely obvious.

'You're cold,' he said softly.

Yeah, completely obvious.

'The water in the jug was from the cooler.'

'So that's the reason…'

All she could do was brazen this out. She tossed her head and met his eyes direct. 'What other reason could there be?'

His lips curved. In his tanned face, his teeth were white and straight and perfect. Actually everything in his face was perfect. And in the dark tee shirt and dark trousers he looked pretty-boy pirate, especially with the slightly too-long hair. The intensity of his scrutiny was devastating and now he'd fixed on one thing—her mouth.

She saw his intention. She felt it in her lips already—the yearning for touch. But even for her that would be insane. She didn't like the way her pulse was zigzagging all over the place. She didn't like the way her body was so willingly bracing for impact.

'Don't add another insult to the list,' she said, trying to regain control over both of them. But the words didn't come out as forcefully as she'd intended. Instead they whispered on barely a breath—because she could barely move enough to breathe.

'How can appreciating beauty be an insult?'

Penny's pulse thundered. She was used to confident men. They were the kind she liked—pretty much bullet proof. But this was more than just superficial brashness; this was innate, absolute arrogance. He stood even closer, filling all her senses. Her blood rushed to all her secret places and left her brain starving of its ability to operate.

His smile suddenly flashed brighter—like how the flame flared on a gas hob when you accidentally twisted the knob the wrong way. His hand lifted and he brushed her lips with a finger. She shivered.

Shock. She was in shock. That was the problem. That was why she wasn't resisting....

His expression heated up all the more. 'You okay?'

'Mmm.'

His traversing finger muffled the words she couldn't speak anyway. She was too busy pressing her lips firmly together to stop herself from opening up and inviting him in. But somehow he got that invite anyway because he lifted his finger and swiftly replaced it with his mouth.

Oh.

It was light. A warm, gentle, coaxing kiss that

promised so much more than it gave. But what it did give was good. He moved closer, not threatening, but with a hint of masculine spice and just enough pressure to make her accept him. To make her want more. Surprised that it wasn't a full-throttle brazen burst of passion, she relaxed. Her eyes automatically closed as her body focused on the exquisite sweetness trickling into her. It had been a long time since she'd felt anything so nice—a subtle magic that melted her resistance, and saw her start to strain for what she knew he was holding at bay.

Her lips parted—she couldn't deny herself. His response came immediate, and powerful. She heard his sound of satisfaction and his hands moved from the steel behind to her soft body. She trembled top to toe as he swiftly shaped her curves, pulling her against him. She had to grab hold of his shoulders or she was going to tumble backwards. The kiss deepened again as she felt the wide, flat planes and hard strength of him. Her neck arched back as he stroked into her mouth. She lifted her hand, sliding her fingers into his thick hair. He showed no mercy then, bending her back all the more as he sought full access, kissing her jaw and neck and back up again to claim her mouth—this time with confident, carnal authority.

She shuddered at the impact, felt him press closer still. Sandwiched between him and the cabinet, she was trapped between forces as unyielding and demanding as each other. Yet she had no desire to escape, not now.

The arrogance of him was breathtaking. But not anywhere as breathtaking as the way he kissed. It was as if he was determined to maximise pleasure for them both and the control she usually held so tight started to slide as her own desire mounted.

He was silk-wrapped steel and she wanted to feel all of him against her, slicing into her. She wanted him. Wanted as she hadn't wanted anyone in a long, long time. Okay, ever. Hungry for his strength and passion, she kissed him back—melting against his body, delving into his mouth with her tongue, so keen to explore more.

And he knew. He lifted his hand from her waist to her breast and, oh, so lightly stroked his fingers across her violently taut nipple.

She felt the touch as if her skin were bare. And it burned too hot.

She jerked back, ripping her mouth free from his. Their eyes met, faces inches apart. A flare of something dangerous kindled in his—different from the earlier fury but just as frightening for Penny. She pushed as far back against the cool metal cabinet as she could, breathing hard. She shook her head, the only method of communication she could manage. While he stood, rock hard, and stared right back at her.

A million half-thoughts murmured in her head—desperate thoughts, forgotten thoughts, *frightening* thoughts.

Carter Dodds wasn't the kind of man to let a woman stay on top—Penny's only acceptable position, metaphorically anyway. He'd just demonstrated he'd always ultimately be the one in charge—his almost pretty-boy packaging disguised a total he-man with all masculine, all dominant virility. He'd made his move that way—lulling her into a sense of sweet security before unleashing his true potency and damn near swamping her reason. She liked sex—enjoyed the chase, the fun of touch, the fleeting closeness. But she never, ever lost control. *She* had to be in charge—*needed* to be the one who was wanted—even if only for that little while. She was very careful with whom she shared her body because she would always walk away. She ensured that a lover understood that. Commitment wasn't something she could ever give. Nor was complete submission. So the sensations now threatening to submerge all her capacity for rational thought were very new. And very unwelcome.

But there was a logical explanation. Less than five minutes ago she'd thought she was being attacked. Her heart hadn't had a chance since to stop its manic stuttering and it was still sending 'escape now' blasts through her blood.

'Well, that was one way to burn off the adrenalin overload.' She totally had to act cool.

'Is that what you were doing?'

'Sure. You know, I was still wired from the fright of you assaulting me in my own office.'

He stepped back, taking his heat with him. But his scrutiny seemed even more intense than ever. 'Oh. So what was it for me?'

She hazarded a simple guess. 'Normal?'

His mouth quirked. 'Not.'

Cool just wasn't happening but she had to scrape her melting body back together. She wasn't afraid of taking fun where it could be found, but there wasn't fun to be had here. Anything that hot eventually had to hurt. And any emotion that intense scared her. In ten minutes with Carter she'd already run the gamut of terror, fury and lust—way too much of the latter. So she turned away from the challenge in his eyes.

'I need to get going. I'm late as it is.' The sooner she got to the bar, the better—she had to burn up the energy zinging round her body like a demented fly trapped in a jar. Fast and free on the dance floor for the next eight hours might do it.

'Hot date?'

'Very.' She lied, happy to slam the brakes on anything between them by invoking her imaginary man friend. She opened up her gym bag; she'd straighten up her appearance and then her insides. But those insides shrieked—she breathed choppily, her heart jack-hammered—so the hairdryer's cacophony was completely wonderful. It muted her clamouring nerves.

Carter took a couple of strides to get himself out of physical range so he could get a grip on the urge to haul her back against him. He didn't know what had got into him. He'd just kissed a complete stranger. A stranger who he'd initially thought was Mason's cheating thief.

He should probably apologise. But how could he be sorry for something so good? Except for a second there she'd looked at him as if he'd struck her, not snogged her. She'd looked shocked and almost hurt, almost vulnerable.

And then she'd blamed that chemistry on adrenalin? Who did she think she was kidding? And now she was apparently late for her *date* and she had her hairdryer blasting. But it wasn't her hair getting the treatment. It was her shirt. She held it out from her body, blowing the warm air over the silk. Then she lifted the nozzle and aimed it down her neckline—what, so she could dry her soft, wet skin? Not helping his raging erection subside any. Nope, that just yanked it even tighter.

A light flickered on her desk. Her mobile. He glanced back up; she was still focused on her shirt. He picked up the mobile to hand it to her, his thumb hit the keypad and, oh, shame, that message from Mel just flicked up on the screen.

Where r u? Kat & Bridge already on d-floor & lookg tragic. Need yr expertise.

Her hot date was with Mel, Kat and Bridge? A bunch of women out on a mission—on a Monday night. That shouldn't amuse him quite as much as it did. He walked up, took the dryer from her hand and pointed it at his wet hair. Immediately he jerked back from the blast of air. 'It's freezing!'

The pink in her cheeks deepened.

'Yeah,' he teased, the sparks arcing between them again. 'I thought you were feeling hot.'

'It's malfunctioning,' she said sulkily.

Carter fiddled with the switch and then aimed the dryer at her like a gun. 'Or maybe it's because you had it turned on cold.'

Boom—even more red blotches peppered her creamy skin. She snatched the appliance back off him and switched it off.

'Here's your phone.' He bit the bullet and handed it over.

She looked at the screen and frowned. 'You read my text?'

'It flashed when I picked it up.' He shrugged almost innocently.

'You didn't need to pick it up.'

'But I like picking up pretty little things.' Even less innocent.

Blacker than black eyes narrowed. 'I'm sure you've had plenty of practice.'

'Well, that does make for perfect performance.' Yep, wickedly sinful now.

'Is that what you think you offer? Perfection?'

He grinned at her tone. She made provocation so irresistible. 'You don't think?'

Her eyes raked him hard and, heaven help him, he loved it. 'I think you could do with some more practice.'

'You're offering?'

She turned away from him, retrieved the jug from the floor and marched to the water cooler to refill it. What, she was literally going to douse the flames again? But, no, she poured the water around the base of the monstrosity that was supposedly an office plant.

'What is it, some kind of triffid?' He reached up to the branches overhanging the cabinet. 'If it grows any more, there won't be room for anyone to work in here.'

'She belongs to Carol and she'll be here when she gets back. All healthy.'

'You think that's really going to happen?' Carter knew Mason's long-time assistant had a cancer battle on her hands. She'd been off for months and Mason was paying her full salary out of his own pocket. Which was why finding the person stealing from him was a priority. He was paying for two PAs. He was a hardworking, generous employer who deserved better than some skunk skimming and putting the entire company in jeopardy.

'Of course she's coming back.' Penny banged the jug back on top of the filing cabinet and finally looked at him directly again. The flames were still there. 'Is someone really stealing from him?'

Carter nodded. 'I think so.'

'But Mason's one of the good guys. He gives so much to charity. He doesn't deserve that.'

'That's why I'm here.'

Her appraisal went rapier sharp. 'Well, you'd better lift your game.'

'Hmm.' He nodded agreeably. 'I was thinking that too.' But the game he meant was the one with her. And he didn't miss the warring desire and antagonism in her expression.

He walked alongside her down the corridor, rode the lift in silent torture. The space between them was too small but he wanted it even smaller—to nothing but skin on skin. Like a tiger, he was ready to pounce. At least his body was; his brain was frantically trying to issue warnings—like he didn't have time for this, like he needed to focus.

The security guard leapt up from his desk to get the door. 'Goodnight, Penny.' His smile widened as he watched her walk across the foyer towards him. That smile faded when he glanced behind her and registered Carter's frown. 'Goodnight, sir.' Suddenly all respectful.

Carter made himself nod and smile.

'Hope Maddie's better when you get home,' Penny said lightly.

'Me too.' The guard's smile spread again. 'See you tomorrow. Not too early, you understand?'

She just laughed as she went through the door.

'Have fun, Penny,' Carter drawled softly as they hit the pavement.

She turned and fluttered him a look one eyelash short of do-me-now. 'Oh, I plan to.'

So she couldn't resist striking the sparks either. And he knew the kind of fun girls like her liked—the eat-men-for-breakfast kind. He smiled, happy to play if she wanted, because experience had made him too tough to chew. She could learn that if she dared.

She walked away, her legs ridiculously long in that sexy strip of a skirt, her balance perfect on the high, narrow heels. Her glossy brown hair cascaded down to her almost too-trim waist. He bet she worked out in the pursuit of perfection. Not that she needed to bother. She nailed it on attitude alone.

Testosterone—and other things—surged again. So did his latent combative nature. That vulnerability he'd seen upstairs when he'd startled her, and again after he'd kissed her? A mirage—she'd been buying time while assessing her position. For Penny the PA knew how to play men—the slayer look she'd just shot him proved it. Mason thought the world of her. The security guy was falling over himself to help her. She'd want to bring Carter to heel like every other man she knew. Yeah, he'd seen her vixen desire for dominance. She thought she could toy with him as some feline would a mouse.

She was so wrong.

But he could hardly wait for her to bring it on.

CHAPTER TWO

PENNY winked at Jed as she walked back into the building just over nine hours later—three of which had been spent dancing and six sort-of sleeping.

'Too early, Penny.' The security guard covered his yawn, clearly barely hanging out the last half-hour before clocking off.

'Too much to do.'

First in for the day, she wanted to get ahead and be fully functioning by the time Mason showed. Definitely by the time Carter Dodds rolled in. The super-size black coffee in her hand would help. But she'd barely got seated when there was movement in her doorway.

'Thought I'd bring this up before I left.'

Jed walked in—well, from the voice she knew it was him. His body was completely obscured by the floral bouquet that was almost too wide to fit through the door.

'They just arrived,' he puffed.

'Not more?' Penny shrivelled deeper into her seat. She knew who they were from. Aaron—a spoilt-for-choice playboy type with several options on the go—the kind of guy Penny always looked for when she needed some company for a while. Only the spark was missing. Last week she'd told him no and goodbye—thought she'd made it clear—but the flowers continued to prove otherwise.

'Thanks, Jed,' she said as he offloaded the oversize blooms onto her desk. 'Have a good sleep.'

'Not me who needs it.'

Penny held back her sigh. She'd take the bunch back down to Reception again but she'd wait 'til Jed had gone for the day—he was exhausted after the night shift and had to go home to a sick preschooler. He didn't need to be hauling flowers back and forth for her.

She picked up her phone and hit one of the pre-programmed buttons.

'SpeedFreaks.'

'Hi, Kate,' Penny said. 'I've got a floral delivery please.'

'Penny? Another one?'

'Yeah.' She tried not to sound too negative about it. It was pretty pathetic to be upset by having masses of flowers delivered; most women would be thrilled. But cut flowers didn't make her think of romance and sweethearts, they made her think hospitals and funerals and lives cut way too short. 'Can you pick them up as soon as possible?'

She heard a movement behind her and turned, smiling in anticipation of Mason. But she forgot all about Mason, or smiling, even the flowers. Only one thing filled her feeble mind.

Tall, broad shoulders, dark hair dangerously leaning towards shaggy—she shouldn't be thinking shag anything. But she was. Because his eyes were leaning towards dangerous to match. She half waved with her phone hand to let him know she was occupied. But he didn't go away and she really needed him to because her head wasn't working well with him watching her like that. She pointedly looked past him to the corridor—didn't he know to come back in a few minutes?

No. He just thudded a heavy shoulder against the door-frame, becoming a human door—blocking her exit and anyone else's entry to the room.

And he smiled. Not just dangerous—positively killer.

She tried to look away, honest she did. But that ability had been stolen from her the moment her eyes had met his.

'Can you get them picked up asap?' she asked on auto, her brain fried by Carter's perfectly symmetrical features. Other parts of her body had gone on quick burn too. Thank heavens she still had her jacket on, because her boobs were like twin beacons screaming her interest through her white blouse. Memories of that gentle stroke last night tormented her. 'They'll be at Reception.'

He was even more handsome in the morning light. Even more now she wasn't blinded by fear and her senses weren't heightened by a surge of adrenalin. No, now it was some other hormone rippling through her body making her shiver.

He stared back as if he were mentally undressing her as fast as she was him. There were no black jeans and tee today, it was suit all the way. Dark, so understated it actually stood out, its uniform style showing off the fat-free frame beneath. Penny's heart thundered.

She turned back to her desk, her voice lowering. 'Thanks, Kate.' She wanted off the phone.

'Are you sure you don't want them? Or him?' Kate didn't pick up on Penny's need-to-hang-up vibe. 'He must be loaded to keep sending you these massive bouquets. And he's obviously dead keen.'

Penny winced. Then winced again as she realised Carter would be able to hear Kate too—the phone volume was too loud. She glanced over her shoulder and jumped. He wasn't in the doorway any more. He was about three inches away—at the most.

'No. I'll spell it out in single syllables.' But Penny tensed. She didn't know how more obvious she could be. She'd thought Aaron would be fine with a few dates' fun before saying goodbye. Only they hadn't got anywhere near that far. She figured the over-the-top floral attention was just him not being used to hearing 'no' and now he was determined to make her change her mind for the boy sport of it. But she couldn't be sure. And because she couldn't be completely sure, she couldn't be completely harsh. Not ever again.

'Where do you want them to go?'

'What about the hospice? But send them to the staff-room. Those guys work so hard.'

'Sure.'

Carter had his ultimate weapon loaded again—that smile was amused now, curving his full, sensual mouth. The green-blue eyes were bright and clear, but the clarity itself seemed to be shielding secrets within. Like a mirror they reflected the surface—and blocked access to the depths behind.

She replaced the receiver and turned to face her shameless eavesdropper full on. She ran her hands down the side of her skirt, pretending to smooth it but really trying to get rid of the clammy feeling.

'You don't want to keep them?' He was far too close

in this spacious office—why couldn't he stay on the far side of her desk?

He inspected the behemoth bunch and looked at the card—the millions of miniature red hearts on the cover obviously showed it was a romantic gift. Somehow him knowing that annoyed her all the more. And he already knew she didn't want them, he'd heard the courier conversation.

'I'm allergic,' she lied through a clamped smile. She wanted to get rid of both the flowers and him. How was she supposed to concentrate when her desk was covered with strong-smelling blooms and a man more gorgeous than the latest Calvin Klein model was making the room shrink more with every breath?

His gaze narrowed. 'Really?'

'Sure.' She blinked. 'I need to get these to Reception.' She reached out to pick up the flowers and escape. But in her haste she scraped her finger against one of the green stems, scratching it. 'Damn.' She looked at her skin and watched the fine white scratch flood with red. Then she glared at the bunch. 'I hate them.'

'Let me see.' He sidestepped the flowers and had her wrist in his hand before her brain could even engage.

Her pulse shot into the stratosphere. 'It's fine. A little plaster or a tissue will stop it,' she babbled faster than a Japanese bullet train rode the rail. Every muscle quivered, wanting him to draw her into a closer embrace.

'Suck on it.' His gaze snared hers. 'Or I will if you want.'

For half a second her jaw hung open. Oh, he was every bit as outrageous in the morning as he was at night. And she was dangerously tickled.

'It's fine.' She snatched her hand back, curling her fingers into a fist. 'I need to get these out of here.'

'Hey.' He frowned and reached out again, pushing her wide gold bangle further up her arm. His frown super-sized up as he stared at the skin he'd exposed. 'Did I do that?'

'Oh.' She glanced down at the purple fingerprint bruises circling her wrist. 'Don't worry about it. I bruise easily.'

He looked back to her face, all the erotic spark in his expression stamped out by concern. 'I'm really sorry.'

'Don't be.' She shook her head quickly. 'Like I said, it's nothing.' Honestly, his contrition just made it worse. She *did* bruise easily and his switching to all serious made him all the more gorgeous. And now he was ever so lightly touching each bruise with a single fingertip.

'It's not fine.'

Penny swallowed. With difficulty. Did he have to be so genuine? She needed to get out of there before she did something stupid like puddle at his feet. That gentle stroking was having some kind of weird hypnotic effect, making her want to move even closer. Instead she turned to the flowers.

'I'll take them.' He picked up the massive bunch with just the one hand.

Okay, that was good because he'd be gone and she'd have a few minutes to bang her head and hormones back together. She should be polite and say something. But she didn't think she had a 'thank you' in her this second. The sensations still reverberated, shaking her insides worse than any earthquake could.

'Penny—'

'Mason should be here any minute,' she said quickly to stave off any more of the soft attention.

'No Mason today,' Carter answered. 'He's working from home. He'll have sent you an email.'

She frowned. Mason never worked from home. He might be eighty but he was almost always first in the door every day. 'I'll take what he needs to him there.' Truthfully she wanted to check on him.

'That would be great.'

Their gazes collided again, only this time the underlying awareness was tempered by mutual concern.

'I'll find out who's hurting him,' Carter said, calmly determined.

Penny nodded.

He cared about the old man, that was obvious. Something jerked deep inside her—the first stirrings of respect and a shared goal.

'I'll be back in a minute.' He swept out of the room.

Penny just sank into her chair.

Carter carried the oversize bunch of blooms down to Reception. Taking the stairs rather than the lift used a bit of the energy coiled in his body, but not enough. Like an overflowing dam he needed a runoff to ease some of the pressure.

Penny had got under his skin faster than snake venom got into a mouse's nervous system. He'd thought about her all night instead of getting his head around the company set-up. Seeing her again today had only made it worse. She looked unbelievably different. The clubbing vixen had vanished and in her place was a perfect vision of conservative and capable. An, oh-so-sensible-length skirt simply highlighted slim ankles and sweet curves, a virginal white blouse was covered by a neatly tailored navy jacket. Hell, there'd even been a strand of pearls at her neck. With her shiny black hair swept back into a plait and her even blacker eyes, she'd looked like the epitome of the nineteen-forties secretary. No matter what she wore, she was beautiful.

Ordinarily Carter wasn't averse to mixing business and pleasure. When business took up so much time, it was sometimes the only way he could find room for pleasure. So long as the woman understood the interest was only ever a temporary thing, and that there were no benefits to the arrangement other than the physical. He didn't generally mix it with someone directly subordinate to him, but someone in one of the offshoot companies or satellite offices.

But he shouldn't mess with Penny—not with only a week or two to find the slimeball ripping Mason off. But he didn't think he was going to be able to work without coming to some kind of arrangement with her, because her challenge was enough to smash his concentration completely. Fortunately he figured she was a woman who'd understand the kind of deal he liked, and the short time frame saved them from any possible messiness. He just had to ensure she understood the benefits—and the boundaries.

In the privacy of the stairwell he opened the card still attached to the flowers.

Hoping to see you again tonight—Aaron.

Carter's muscles tightened. Had she seen him last night? Maybe she had had a hot date after meeting up with the women. Had she gone to this Aaron with the taste of Carter still on her? Because he could still taste her—hot, fresh, hungry.

He wasn't in the least surprised to think she'd go to another guy having just blown hot for him; he was well used to women who manipulated, playing one man off against another. His ex had done exactly that—trying to force him into making a commitment by making him jealous. It hadn't worked. And he sure as hell wasn't feeling jealous now. The aggro sharpening his body this minute was because of the threat to Mason. Not Penny.

He stalked out to Reception and put the flowers on the counter. 'I think a courier company is coming to pick these up.'

The receptionist grinned as she looked at them. 'Penny sent them down?' She shook her head. 'That's the third bunch this week. She's mad not to want them.'

The third this week? It was only Tuesday. Yeah, she would like holding the interest of multiple men. His long-held cynicism surged higher—there was no doubt Penny was as greedy and needy as every other woman he'd known.

It was almost an hour before Carter reappeared, a piece of paper in his hand and a frown creasing his brow. 'Penny, I need you to—'

He broke off as her phone started ringing.

She shrugged an apology and answered it. 'Nicholls Finance, Penny speaking.'

'Did you get the flowers?'

'Aaron,' she whispered, inwardly groaning. She darted a look at Carter, then turned away on her chair so he wouldn't see the flush rising in her cheeks. She already knew he was rude enough to stay and listen. Her best option was to end the call asap. 'It really isn't convenient to talk right now—'

'Did you get them?'

'Yes, I'm sorry, I should have called but it's been a busy morning.' And she could hardly let him down without some privacy. 'Can I call you back?'

'The roses reminded me of you. Stunningly beautiful but with some dangerous prickles.'

Yes, she'd encountered one of those real prickles. She shrank more into her chair. 'Look, it was lovely of you but—'

'Dinner tonight. No excuses.'

She breathed in and tried to stay calm. 'That's a nice idea but—'

'I've already made the reservations. It's my only night off this week and I want to spend it all with you.'

'Aaron, I'm sorry but—'

The phone was taken out of her hand.

'Look, mate, don't bother. She has a new boyfriend and she's allergic to flowers. She's already sent them on to the hospice down the road.'

Penny stared as Carter leaned across her desk. She couldn't hear what Aaron said in response— she could hardly process what Carter had just said so complacently.

'Yeah, I know. Save your dough. It isn't going to happen.' Carter hung up the phone and then looked at her coolly. 'So, I was saying I need you to track down some files for me.'

For a moment she was too shocked to fully feel the rising fury. But then it truck-slammed into her. '*What* did you just do?'

Carter met her gaze with inhuman calm. 'Solved your problem. He won't bother you again.'

'How could you do that?'

'Easily. And you should have done it sooner already. Your body language said one thing, your mouth another. You looked like you wanted to hide under your desk for fear he'd appear, but you were brushing him off too gentle. A guy like that doesn't get subtle, Penny. You need the sledgehammer approach.'

'I didn't need you to be the sledgehammer.' She shook her head. 'That was bully behaviour.'

'It was man talking to man,' he argued with an eye-roll for added effect. 'And more honest than the drivel coming out of your mouth.'

'I was handling him,' she said defensively.

'You were *playing* with him.' Now he didn't sound so calm. Now he sounded that little bit nasty.

Her hands shook as she brushed her hair behind her ear. She hadn't been playing with Aaron, she'd been trying to be nice.

'Three bunches of flowers this week already, isn't it, Penny? You're not even honest enough to tell him you don't want *them*, let alone that you don't want *him*.'

Because she didn't want to be rude. She never wanted to hurt anyone. Never. Horrified tears prickled her eyes as she panicked over Aaron's reaction to Carter's heavy-handedness.

'Why are you so upset?' He stepped closer, his eyes narrowing. 'Oh, I get it. You liked to leave him hanging? Was it good for your ego? You like getting all the flowers and attention? You're a tease.'

'I'm not.' She jerked up out of her chair, beyond hurt at the words he'd just used.

'You are,' he argued. 'Why else wouldn't you cut him free sooner?'

'I tried.' She snatched the paper off him and marched

to the filing cabinet, hauling the drawer open with a loud bang.

'That wasn't trying.' He followed and faced her as she rummaged through the files. 'You're not stupid, Penny. You could have flicked him off much sooner.'

'Maybe I'm not as arrogant or as rude as you are.' She slapped files on the top of the steel. 'I don't like trampling on people's feelings.'

'You don't think it's worse to string him along so your ego can be inflated some more?'

'That wasn't what I was doing.' She crossed her arms in front of her chest.

'Oh, don't tell me you really liked him?' He looked stunned. 'Were you just making life hell for him? Playing with him so he'd do anything you ask him to?'

'Of course not!' She clenched her teeth. 'I was trying to make it clear that nothing was going to happen. I thought I had already. But he didn't deserve your kind of in-your-face humiliation.'

'What he doesn't deserve is you screwing him up and spitting him out only when you're sick of chewing him over.'

Breathing hard, she glared at him as fury burned along her veins. 'Wow, you think so highly of me, don't you, Carter?'

His shoulders lifted in a mocking shrug. 'If you really wanted rid of him, you needed to be cruel to be kind.'

'Well, I'm not cruel,' she said painfully. 'I won't ever be.'

He glared right back at her—for what felt like hours. Slowly she became aware of their isolation in the office, the smallness of the space between them. They were just about in exactly the position they'd been in last night.

'How about honest, then, can you manage that?' he asked quietly.

'Not if it's going to really hurt someone,' she muttered. Utterly honest.

'No.' He shook his head. 'That's the coward's way out.'

Well, what would he know about anything? For all his cruel-to-be-kind cliché, she'd bet her last cent he'd never hurt anyone the way she once had.

She blinked back her sudden tears, focused on his eyes instead. Close up now she saw even more colours in them—not just green and blue but shots of gold as well. All of a sudden she was trying really, really hard not to think of that kiss and how incredible she'd felt. Trying really, really hard not to notice how his mouth looked fuller today.

The atmosphere changed completely. It seemed he'd forgotten his anger too. But there was no less emotion in the air—it just transformed and intensified as it swirled around them. Somehow it made her feel even worse than when he'd been so rude on the phone. Somehow she was more afraid. She couldn't move, couldn't speak.

'Do you want me to kiss you again, Penny?' he asked. 'Is that the real problem here?'

That brought her voice back. 'You are so conceited.'

'So you really can't do honesty,' he jibed.

She bent her head and fished for the last few files, needing to find her moxie more than the damn data. He so easily tipped her balance, she needed her defensive sass back. But all she could manage now was the silent treatment.

'So what should that guy have sent you—a big box of Belgian chocolates?' His tone lightened.

'I don't eat chocolate,' she said shortly, not looking up.

'Maybe you should, smooth off some of those sharp edges. Isn't chocolate better than sex?'

'You're obviously not doing it right if the women you know say that.'

He yelped a little laugh. 'Throw out a challenge, why don't you?'

She slammed the file drawer shut.

'And now you're backing away from it again. See, you *are* a tease. You just like having men want you.'

She faced him full on, to put him firmly in his place. Oh, so arrogant Carter Dodds could definitely cope with that—he wasn't exactly crushable. 'You wanting me is not a compliment.'

'You don't think?' He grinned. 'Well, I'm not going to chase after you with a billion flowers or calls. If you want to follow through on this, just let me know.'

'And you'll come running?'

He shook his head. 'I don't run after any woman.'

'Because they all fall at your feet?'

'Much like the men do at yours, darling,' he murmured. 'But I already know how much you want me so maybe I'll make you beg for it.'

'Cold day in hell, Carter.'

'Don't protest too much, you'll only regret it later.'

She held a breath for a sanity-saving moment. 'You always get everything you want?'

'I already have everything I want. Anything extra is purely for fun.' His lips curved so slowly and his eyes twinkled with such a teasing expression she fought hard not to let her lips move in response. They wanted to smile all of their own accord. To mirror the magic in his smile. How could she want to smile when she was mad with him?

Because the fact was, he was honest—and, yes, more honest than her. He might be teasing but he wasn't saying anything that wasn't a bit true.

'Admit it, you love the fun of it.' Both his eyes and voice invited.

'The fun of what?'

'Flirting.'

'Is that what you're doing?'

'That's what *we've* been doing from the moment we saw each other.'

'Oh, please.' This wasn't *flirting*, this was a full-scale, high-impact, brazen sexual hunt. There was nothing subtle about it.

'You can't deny it,' he said. 'You like what you see. I like what I see.'

She dropped her gaze. Yes, that was all it was. A superficial animal attraction—based on instinct and what the eye found beautiful. They were each a pleasing example of the opposite sex with whom to practise procreation.

'That doesn't mean we should do anything about it. You need to concentrate, you've got a job to do here.' And she needed him to give her some breathing space.

'And I'll do it well. Doesn't mean I can't have a few moments of light relief here and there.'

Light relief was all she ever did. But she didn't think Carter would walk as lightly over her as she would him. 'You don't think this is a distraction?'

'I think it's more of a distraction not to give in to it.'

'Oh, right, so really I should be saying yes for Mason's sake.'

He chuckled. 'You should be saying yes because you can't keep saying no—not to this.'

He had the sledgehammer thing down pat.

She'd known many cocky guys. Had heard many lines—hell, she'd even delivered a few herself. But while Carter was confident, she could also tell he meant every word—and not in some deluded way. He really wanted her. And the truth was, she wanted him too—but to a degree too scary. This kind of extreme just couldn't be healthy.

He leaned a little closer and, despite her caution, Penny couldn't help mirroring his movement. She had to part her lips just that tiny fraction—to breathe, right?

He smiled wickedly and lifted his head away again, his eyes dancing with the delight of a devil. He picked up the files she'd thumped on the top of the cabinet. 'I'll see you at the bar later.'

'You're going tonight?' She whirled away to hide the sudden rush of blood to her face. Oh, yeah, all her blood rushed at the thought of him being there.

'Good opportunity to meet and mingle with the staff socially.'

She could hear his smile as he answered. But she frowned, forgetting her feelings about spending social time with him and thinking of Mason instead. 'I can't believe any of them could be stealing.'

'Greed. You never know who has what addiction, what need that'll push them past moral boundaries.'

'But it's not William.' It was the analyst's last day; he was heading overseas to take on the financial markets in Singapore. 'It couldn't be him.'

'I'm checking everyone,' Carter answered, suddenly cool. 'As he's leaving, I'm checking his deals first.'

Penny went straight to the bathroom and spent several minutes touching up her face—pressing powder over her forehead, cheeks and chin with deliberate, dispassionate dabs. She concentrated on her lipstick, not letting her mind think of her mouth as anything other than a colouring-in challenge—certainly not a hungry bundle of nerve endings yearning to feel the pressure of Carter's mouth on hers again.

But then she stared at her surface-repaired reflection. Was he right? Had she been stringing Aaron along? She hated the way Carter had spoken to him but had she been any better? She could have made it clearer—interrupted him and spoken firmly. Only she had that memory, when she'd inflicted so much pain. It was why she was always so careful to establish the ground rules before she entered any kind of affair now. It was why her affairs were so few and far between and super-brief. She had to be careful because she couldn't handle anything more than easy. Anything more than carefree. No pain, just frivolity and superficial pleasure. She enjoyed sex. She didn't have it anywhere near often enough despite her many nights out dancing, preferring to keep safe in all kinds of ways. But this attraction to Carter was the most extreme thing she'd ever experienced.

He'd offered all she wanted—only the physical—no strings, no messiness. There was certainly no fledgling friendship there, not when he obviously thought she was a manipulative tease. She saw how he looked at her, as if she made him as angry as much as she turned him on. Well, she knew exactly how he felt.

But her reaction to him was too strong to be safe. When emotions were out of control, people got hurt. She wasn't hurting anyone or being hurt ever again. That was her one hard-and-fast rule. And this attraction threatened every ounce of control she had—therefore was too dangerous to engage.

But he was absolute temptation.

She shook her head, overruling her warring instincts. He wasn't *that* overwhelming. Her attraction to him was simply a case of it having been too long. Of course she swooned for tall, dark and handsome, any other red-blooded female would too. Except Carter didn't just have those three attributes, he also had a carefree lack of cut to his hair, wicked brilliance in his eyes and the devil in his smile....

Ugh. She turned her back on the mirror and walked out. He was just incredibly over-confident. He probably wouldn't even deliver on the promise he exuded. Because in truth, for Penny, no man delivered.

CHAPTER THREE

'CHAMPAGNE please.' Nine hours of work and thirty lengths of the pool later, Penny had changed into her clubbing gear, heel-tapped her way into the bar and been served ahead of eight people already queued there.

'So you're friends with the bartenders.'

'And the DJs.' She took her glass and turned to face Carter. 'And the bouncers,' she added with just that little bit of emphasis.

His grin flashed. 'Really? I thought you didn't like bullies tossing people out of your life.'

He was dressed in the dark casual again. The edginess suited him better.

She sipped the champagne and pretended she had all the chutzpah she'd ever need. 'There's always the exception, Carter.'

'Oh, that there is.' His brows lifted as he looked over every inch of her second-favourite-ever skirt and then her shirt. 'So this is your hunting ground.' He glanced dispassionately at the dance floor. 'Little loud, isn't it?' He grinned evilly. 'How can you get to know someone properly when you can't hear them talk?'

She sidled another inch along the bar and whispered

in his ear. 'By getting close.' She quickly pulled back when she felt him move.

His hand did lift, but all he did was deposit his glass on the bench behind her. Empty already meant he'd been there awhile and he hadn't had trouble catching the attention of the bar staff either.

Penny searched and spotted her workmates over near their usual corner, some already on the dance floor. Safety in numbers. 'Coming to join the others?'

'If I must.'

She deliberately misunderstood his reluctance. 'You don't like to dance?'

He shrugged.

'You've got no rhythm?' she asked totally overly sweetly.

He took her glass from her and sipped carefully. 'I can hold my own.'

'Really.' She didn't try to hide the dare in her tone.

He turned to face her. There were probably over a hundred and fifty people present, but suddenly there was only him. 'I'm happy to watch for a while first. That's what you want, isn't it? To be watched? That's why you dress like this.' His fingers brushed the hem of her skirt and slipped onto her bare skin.

She took her glass back off him. 'I dress like this because I don't like to get too hot. And so I can move easily.'

'Yeah, real easy.' All innuendo.

Swallowing some sweet fizzing bubbles, she smiled. 'Not jumping to all the wrong conclusions again, are you?'

'No, I'm examining the details and evaluating in a reasoned manner.' His finger traced slowly back and forth over a two-inch stretch of her thigh and, despite the heat of the late summer night and the press of too many people, goose bumps rose.

'Like you did last night?'

'I admit my naturally suspicious instinct overruled my usual close observation. At first.'

'So you admit you were wrong?'

'I already have. And I already apologised. Last night. Stop trying to milk it—we can move on, you know.' He took her glass from her again. 'Or are you too scared to?'

She bit the inside of her lip as he smiled and sipped more of her champagne, intently watching her reaction. He wasn't kidding about the close observation.

'You know we want the same thing.'

'Maybe, maybe not,' she hedged.

'Definitely.'

'All I want right now is to dance.' *With him.* But she had to hold some secrets close.

His grin flared. 'Precisely my point.'

She turned her back on him, positively strutted to where half the others from the office were already getting their groove on. That was one of the things she liked about the company—the really healthy party scene that went with it. They worked hard and played every bit as hard and, despite those thirty lengths already, she still had too much energy to burn. William and some of the other guys joined in and the floor got crowded. Her blood zinged. Yeah, this was what she needed; easy-going freedom and fun.

The music *was* loud—which she liked—the beat both fast and steady. But it wasn't long before she turned her head. Because it wasn't one-way traffic—she wanted to watch him too. She met his stare full on across the floor. For that split second she saw how easily he read her—piercing right into her head to find out exactly what she wanted.

He walked straight towards her.

And, yes, that was exactly what she wanted.

Carter and William were a similar height but Carter drew all attention away from the other man. His aura and his physique commanded it. Broader in the shoulders, bigger, stronger—yes, she was totally going cave-girl, her body instinctively turning towards the male who seemed likely to offer the best protection.

His smile wasn't exactly safe, though. And other instincts were warring with her basic sexual ones—shrieking that getting closer to Carter would be no protection at all. But that look in his eyes mesmerised her again. She couldn't move—like prey frozen in the path of the predator. Not safe at all. But then, at this moment, she didn't want to be.

His hand slid round her back and he pulled her against him, his head descending so quickly she didn't even have a chance to blink. But there was no kiss for her hungry mouth; he was too clever for that. It was the slightest brush on her jaw, so quick and light she wondered if it had just been her desperate imagination. Her breath escaped in a rough sigh of disappointment and then she inhaled—all excitement again as he pulled her that bit tighter to him. Now she was wholly in his arms, her chest pressed to his, his hand wide and strong splaying across her spine, his other lifting to stroke down her plait, tugging at the end of it to tilt her face back up to his.

But she avoided his all-seeing eyes. Turned to look over his shoulder instead. Her workmates' eyes were bugging out. She was definitely breaking a few conventions tonight; she didn't ever dance this close to anyone in the office. But then Carter wasn't officially on the payroll. And in less than a second she didn't care what they were thinking anyway because the impact of his proximity hit her and *she* could no longer think. She couldn't do anything but move with him.

He said nothing, didn't need to, merely moved his hands to guide her where he wanted—natural dancer, natural leader, natural lover. All easy rhythm. And she turned to plasticine just like that.

Chest to breast, hands to shoulder and waist, thigh brushing thigh—but eyes not meeting. The need to deny the madness built in her chest. But he was totally taking advantage of the flickering lights and the crowd of people to crush her closer still. His sledgehammer style—steamrolling over her caution just by being himself.

The feelings intensified. She wasn't comfortably warm any more but unbearably hot. She couldn't breathe either—he always made her so damn breathless, made her heart beat too fast, made her brain go vacant.

She wanted to rest her head on his shoulder for a moment, wanted to escape the crowds and the claustrophobic feeling choking her. She wanted to move slowly with him. Even more she wanted time to stop—to leave her pressed mindlessly against him with no pressure of the past to bear on her.

But that was impossible. And this discomfort was so wrong. Dancing was where she felt the best, the most free. She liked it fast and loud, but now it was only his heartbeat she could hear—strong and regular and relentless—and it scared her. Her own heart thundered, scaring her.

Why was she stumbling, why were her eyes watering, blinded by the flashing lights?

She had to escape. Pushing away from him, she took a deep breath to try to stop from drowning in the sensations. She listened for the beat again. She needed to be alone and unrestricted—alone in the crowd.

She turned, saw William only a couple of feet away. She moved towards him, welcoming the break from Carter. Breathing deeper, more calmly. Yes, she needed recovery time to get her grip back.

William was a handsome guy, easily the best-looking man in the office until Carter had arrived, but there was none of that crazy swimming feeling in her head that she had when dancing with Carter. She had no trouble breathing, or thinking or staying in control of her own body. This made so much more sense.

Manageable.

She breathed deep again and smiled at him. William smiled back. This was better.

Carter stood on the dance floor and watched her spin in some other guy's arms. William. The guy whose work he'd just spent the afternoon cross-checking—and it was all clear. That didn't stop the surge of hatred from rising. Despicable, unwanted, violent.

His fists curled. There was no hope of recovering his calm, not now he'd felt the way she moved against him—all fluid grace and perfect rhythm and soft freedom. All he could think of was her supple body sliding against his as she danced with him intimately. Every muscle ached for the intense release they'd share.

But there she was going from him to another in a heartbeat. Any other woman and he'd roll his eyes and walk away. He made it a rule never to care enough to be bothered by a woman's games. But he had to get out of there before he punched that William guy in the face. And it wasn't even his fault. Penny was the player, not him.

Carter wasn't into violence and the wave of aggression he felt made him even more angry—with himself. He'd punish his own body instead, take it out on the rowing machine or the treadmill or the punchbag that were in the gym down the stairs from his serviced apartment. He'd go there and sweat it out right now.

Raw lust was his problem, and he'd felt nothing like it in his life. So what that she was attractive? There were millions of pretty women in the world—that didn't mean his body had to start acting as if Penny were the only one that could switch him on. It had been a while, that was all, too many hours on the job and not enough off socialising. But maybe seeing her in that half-wet top last night had put some spell on him, because all he could think about was getting her naked. Her and only her.

Well, he'd get over it.

He walked out of the bar, knowing he'd probably just caused a massive stir and a ton of gossip, given he hadn't bothered to speak to any others on the staff. Still, better for them to be gasping over his sex life than his real reason for being there. It provided good distraction in terms of his cover.

But for him, it was an absolute nightmare. Penny's accusation this morning had been on target. She was more than a distraction, she was catastrophic for his concentration, and he couldn't let sexual hunger affect the job he was doing for Mason. He'd commandeered an office on the floor below so he wouldn't even see her during work hours unless it was absolutely necessary, but it wasn't enough. Not when he was hunting her out at night. There was only one way forward—he had to forget her and just get on with the job. She could toy with that other guy. He damn well didn't care.

CHAPTER FOUR

PENNY felt as if she'd overdosed on no-doze. Her heart hammered, she fidgeted. Hyper-alert, she watched every second, hoping he'd hurry up and come say hi. But he didn't. Minutes dragged like decades. Mason had emailed in again to say he'd spend another day working at home. Maybe Carter was with him. Or maybe he was locked in his office down the stairs. She wasn't going to go see. She wasn't going to waste another minute wondering where he was or why he'd done the vanishing act last night. And she certainly wasn't going to regret the fact that he had.

Eventually she went out for a power walk. Fresh air might help her regain her equilibrium and stop her from doing all those things she'd told herself she wasn't going to do.

Twenty minutes later she walked back into the building, even more hot and edgy. As the automatic door slid shut behind her Carter stepped out of the lift. He didn't hesitate when he saw her, just strode straight across the foyer like a man possessed.

'Did you enjoy the rest of your night?' he asked, still ten paces away.

'Yes,' she said brightly. She'd hated it. She'd danced

and danced until she couldn't fake it any more and gone home to stare at the ceiling.

'Really?' Now he looked angry and he lengthened his stride even more.

A rabbit in the headlights, Penny failed to leap out of his path. And all of a sudden he did what she'd wanted him to do less than twelve hours ago—yanked her close—one hand round her waist, his other pulling her plait so she was forced to tilt her head back. Not that he needed to force it, because she melted right into him. For hours in the early morning she'd lain half asleep, dreaming of this. Now she wasn't sure if she was still dreaming—and only by clinging, by putting her palm to that sharp jaw could she be sure that he was real and kissing her hot and rough and right in the middle of Reception.

Her groan caught in her mouth as he plundered. How could she ever say no to this? She was lost to it, utterly lost.

But just as suddenly he pulled away.

'You're still hungry.' His words whispered low and angry.

Stunned, she stared. And by the time she got herself together enough to say something, he'd already gone out of the door behind her.

Her anger hit. What the hell did he think he was doing, carrying on like that in public? Thank heaven no clients had been waiting for appointments. Only the receptionist was there, though that meant everyone in the company would know about it by now—she'd have emailed them already. Not that they'd be surprised after the dirty dancing display last night. Penny ground her teeth. Yes, it was a good thing she was going soon because things were getting more than a little untidy. She marched up the stairs and felt even more hot and furious by the time she got to the top.

Files, she'd sort out the wretched files. She stomped over to the cabinet and slid the drawer open, pointlessly checking all the contents were in the right order. Which they were—but the perfectionist in her just had to be sure.

'Got you some tea to calm your nerves,' Carter said smoothly.

She whirled fast to face him. Stepped so close, so quick, he actually took a step back and deposited the steaming cup on the nearest flat surface—the top of the cabinet. She moved closer still, keeping the scarcest of centimetres between them.

'I don't fool around at work, Carter.' She furiously whispered in his face, using anger to hide both the turmoil raging inside her and the desire he'd roused so effortlessly. 'Don't embarrass me like that again.'

His hands whipped round her, pulling her flush against him. Letting her know how lethally he was turned on. Her nerves shook beneath her skin, her muscles melted—only to reform even tighter and aching to feel his impression.

'You liked it, Penny.' His hand firmly cupped her butt, pulling her yet closer against his thick erection. 'You liked it as much as I did.'

She had and she did nothing to deny it now, did nothing to pull away from the searing embrace. If anything she melted that millimetre more into him. There could be no denying the force of it. She gasped as he thrust his hips harder against her—his expression told her he knew it all. But he was angry too.

'Who was it who ended that kiss, Penny? Who was it who pulled back?' His smile was a snarl. 'If it had been up to you we'd be sweaty and catching our breath right about now. If we'd been alone you'd have let me do anything. And you'd just about be ready to go for round two.'

Her blood beat through her with such force she felt dizzy. 'Well, then, what the hell were you thinking making that move *there*?'

He held still for a moment, and although his body remained rock hard she felt the anger drain away from him. The next second he actually laughed. 'I wasn't thinking. Isn't that obvious?'

Shaking his head ruefully, he looked up above them. 'Here we are again. I'm starting to think this plant is like some kind of magic mistletoe.'

'You always have the urge to kiss me when you're under it?' The urge to flash him a look was irresistible.

'I always have the urge to kiss you, full stop.'

Admittedly he didn't sound that thrilled about it, but even so a spurt of pleasure rippled through her. It was good he wanted her like that. It evened the score. She leaned back against the filing cabinet and looked at him, feeling as if she'd done her warm-up and was ready for the race—excited, a little nervous, full of anticipation.

Carter stepped forward, closing the gap until he was fully pressed against her again. His blue-green gaze devoured her features. She wished he'd just hurry up and kiss her. She put her palm to his jaw again, unable to resist just that small touch.

'Go on, Penny.' Ragged-voiced, he dared her. 'Deal with me.'

Their mouths hovered, barely a millimetre apart, hot

breath mingling with even hotter desire. How could she possibly resist? She opened her mouth that little more.

'Well,' a deep voice sounded. 'Looks like I finally get to meet him.'

Penny leapt a clear foot, or she would have if Carter hadn't had such a grip on her—a grip that suddenly tightened.

'Matt,' she squeaked. Wide-eyed, she stared past Carter at the tall figure standing beside her desk.

'I've heard so much about you but I didn't think I'd get to meet you.' Matt walked closer, his too-intelligent eyes nailing Carter and then flicking to her. 'Penny, you didn't tell us he actually worked with you.'

She was still trying to wriggle out of Carter's grip but he'd tightened it even more to pinch-point. 'Yes,' she managed to say softly but Matt didn't hear her.

'You're him, right?' Matt asked Carter direct. 'The "man" she keeps emailing about—the one who dines and dances and takes her away every weekend.'

Penny wanted the world to open up and suck her under right this second. Because what would Carter think about that lot of detail? What would Matt think when he found out the truth?

She looked into Carter's eyes, saw the blues and greens and ice-cold anger out in equal doses. She pressed against him just that little more, softening herself in the hopes he'd also soften. Okay, she was pleading as she, oh, so slightly nodded her head at him, all but begging with her eyes.

But Carter felt as if he were made of rock as he rubbed one fist across his lips. He seemed to see into her soul with his bleak, penetrating glare. She waited for the axe to fall. Carter wanted her but he didn't think much of her, she knew that. So he wasn't about to come riding to her rescue now.

And Matt, impossibly tall and grown-up Matt, was waiting for an answer.

'Yes,' Carter finally said. 'I'm that man.'

In shocked relief Penny softened against Carter completely, but felt every one of his muscles flinch.

'I'm Matt Fairburn, Penny's brother.' Matt flashed one of his rare smiles and held out his hand.

An infinitesimal hesitation and Carter reached out too. 'Carter Dodds, Penny's man.'

It was a firm handshake, Penny could tell. It went on that half-second too long, as if they were testing each other's muscles and manliness or something. Which was ridiculous, because last time she'd seen Matt he'd still been half-boy, half-man. The intense student too focused and serious for his own good. But now he was…different. Now he was assessing, and judging—just as he wanted to do in his career.

She took the opportunity of their formal introductions to extricate herself from the rock and the hard place she was literally squashed between. Emotionally, she was even more caught.

'What are you doing here, Matt?' She summoned a big smile as she asked, because she had a fictional happy life to live up to.

'Coming to make sure you'll be around to have dinner with me. Has to be tonight because I've got a conference for the next couple of days.'

She hadn't known he was in town. Why hadn't he emailed to tell her? 'Of course I can do dinner,' she said brightly.

'No other plans?' he asked.

'None I can't change.'

Matt's brows lifted. 'What about the man?' He turned to Carter. 'You'll come too, right? I want to grill you. Being the only one in the family to meet you so far, I've got responsibilities to those back home. Namely Mum.'

He spoke casually but Penny understood the undertone. Her kid brother was checking up on her. She tried to make her muscles relax but her smile felt superglued on. 'Carter has to work tonight. Sorry, Matt. He has a meeting.'

'Actually, honey, that one got cancelled.' Carter tucked a strand of her hair behind her ear as if he had all the rights of such casual intimacy. 'That's what I was coming to tell you only I got…distracted.' He looked from her eyes to her mouth in a blatant sensual stamp and then he turned. 'I'd love to be there, Matt.'

All Penny's internal organs shrank. 'But—'

'You can let me know for sure later,' Matt broke in, his expression impassive. 'I have to see your flat too, Penny. More of Mum's orders.'

'You should have warned me.' Penny laughed. 'I'd have tidied up.'

Matt answered with a quick rare smile again, but Carter wasn't smiling at all.

'I'll walk you out,' Penny said quickly, wanting to take charge of the plans without Carter listening in. She manufactured more brightness as she led him to the lift. 'Why didn't you tell me you were coming sooner? I could have made some plans.'

'Wanted to surprise you.'

Yeah, he was checking up. She hated that he felt he had to do that. Her little brother had had to grow up too soon and he'd got all paternal and protective on her. It was her fault. He should be out there having wild times of his own, not worrying about her or carrying the burden of their parents' worry for her. And that was her fault too. She'd tried to ease it—hence her stupid, overly imaginative emails.

But now she smiled and gave him a hug. 'It's so awesome to see you. I'll text you with details of where to meet, okay?'

'You mean you actually have my number?' Matt asked dryly. 'I wondered.'

Yeah, it was only the occasional email that she sent. She rarely texted, and never talked. It was easier that way. She'd never said she was brave. And she was feeling beyond cowardly now. She went back into the lift and reluctantly pushed the button for the top. Droplets of discomfort sweat slicked her skin yet she felt chilled to the bone.

Carter stood by the windows in Mason's office, looking down at the street scene below. She closed the door behind her and waited.

After a moment that made her nerves stretch past break point, he turned.

'Just how many men have you got on the go, Penny?'

She shook her head. Glad his desk was between her and him. Because he was looking more than a little angry and she needed all four feet of solid wood between them.

'Tell me about him.' Carter's voice lifted. 'He's some sugar daddy you spend the weekends with?'

Her flush deepened. 'No.'

'No?'

Penny swallowed the little pride she had left. 'I made him up.'

Carter blinked. 'Pardon?'

'I made him up. In my emails home, I invented a relationship.'

For the first time she saw Carter at a loss for words— momentarily. His eyes narrowed and he took a couple of steps closer. 'You're telling me this "man" doesn't exist? You don't actually have a real boyfriend.'

'No.'

'And there's no one you're dating, or sleeping with, or friends with benefits or whatever you care to call it.'

She held his gaze. 'I'm not seeing anyone at the moment. No.'

He nodded slowly. 'When were you last seeing someone?'

'It's been a few months.' She was flushed with heat— anger, embarrassment and the burning need for him to believe her. For some stupid reason it was important he understand. 'I don't remember exactly how long.'

'But Aaron doesn't count?'

She lifted her chin and answered pointedly. 'A couple of kisses don't count.'

Carter's jaw went more angular. 'So how many kisses haven't you counted in the last few months?'

Her brows shot up. 'Aaron. Another guy. You.'

'My kisses don't count?' he asked softly.

'Definitely not.'

His devil grin flashed. 'I've figured it out.'

Penny blinked at his suddenly bright demeanour. 'Figured what out?'

'How to tell when you're lying.'

She jerked. 'What? How?'

He shook his head and laughed aloud. 'Not telling because then you'll stop doing it.'

'Stop doing what?' She sighed and gave up, knowing he wasn't about to spill it. Besides, there was something more important to know. 'You do believe me, don't you?'

He went serious again. 'Yeah, I do.'

She was absurdly relieved. She'd been a complete fool with the emails and he knew it, but oddly that didn't matter so long as he believed her when she told the truth.

He walked around his desk, picked up her hand and ran a light finger over the bruises still marking her wrist. 'You know I just said that about coming to dinner tonight to wind you up...make up whatever excuse.' He gave her an ironic glance. 'You've got the experience. Your brother might not know your little giveaway.'

Penny frowned and pulled her hand free.

Dinner with Matt. She'd half forgotten it in her need to clear up the confusion with Carter. But now she thought about it, she was dreading it already—the questions, the search for conversation, all the anxiety... She just didn't want to face it. She'd spent years not facing it.

Actually maybe it would be a good idea to have someone with her. With extra company she could present the happy façade for the night, no problem. And she really was happy. It was just that she'd added an imaginary gorgeous man to give the picture a fully glossy finish. Companionship without complications— she had enough complications inside already. It had been so long since her last real, short-term gorgeous man, she'd invented one.

Now she looked at Carter. Handsome, charming, socially expert Carter.

'I think you should come with me,' she said.

His brows shot up.

'No, I mean it.' She stepped in closer to him. 'Come to dinner. After all, Matt's expecting you now.'

His attention dropped to her body and back up. 'Well, isn't that your problem for misleading him in the first place?'

'But you played up to it. The least you can do is follow through.'

Carter leaned back against the edge of his desk, a small smile tweaking his mouth.

Really, the more Penny thought about it, the better an idea it was. Matt could maybe learn a few things from Carter—social smoothness for one. And Carter would deflect the attention off herself. She didn't know how well she could maintain the façade on her own. Most importantly, the conversation would stay in safe waters. Matt wouldn't drag up the past with Carter present.

'I've seen you talking with the guys who work here... And the girls.' Her gaze narrowed. 'You're good socially.'

Too good actually. Every woman looked at him as if he were the biggest honeypot to hit the town in a decade or forty—and they all wanted a taste.

'Is that a compliment? Because the way you're talking I'm not sure...' He studied her slyly.

She couldn't hold back her smile. He was a charming wretch and he knew it.

'Come to dinner with me,' she leant forward to whisper. 'Be my pretend man.'

Carter's blood was still burning from the horror of

seeing her dance with someone else last night. He wasn't a hypocrite—he didn't expect women to have less experience than him, but the thought of her being in bed with another guy had made his stomach acid boil. The foreign jealousy rotted him from the inside out and he badly needed to ditch it. He'd spent all night awake wondering if she'd taken William home. And despite his vow to forget her, when he'd seen her in Reception this afternoon the urge had hit. He'd had to touch and find out—something, anything—like an animal scenting out a threat. So completely caveman and so unlike his usual carefree style.

And now, now the relief in knowing she hadn't was making him positively giddy, because here he was about to say yes to the most stupid suggestion he'd heard in ages. But he was too intrigued not to. 'Why did you make him up?'

Her gaze dropped. 'I wanted everyone back home to think I'm happy.'

Was she not happy? 'And you have to have a boyfriend to prove that?'

'No,' she said quickly. 'I have a great life—great job, I travel lots. But the man was the icing for them. I know they worry I'm lonely.'

Which she wasn't, of course. She had thousands of adoring suitors. She could have a man every night of the week if she wanted. But it was interesting that she didn't want that. It was interesting that she wanted to kiss *him*.

'So you want me to be the icing?' he croaked. Because if that meant she'd use her tongue on him, he was so happy to oblige.

She tossed her head back. 'It's what we're all supposed

to want, isn't it? Someone who cares, who holds you, who's there for you. Companionship, commitment. Happy ever after. That whole cliché.'

She thought wanting a life partner was a cliché? Hell, where had she been all this time? Because he didn't want a life partner either. He just wanted some uncomplicated fun. 'But that's not what you actually want for yourself?'

He could see the goose bumps on her arms as she recoiled. She really only wanted a lover for a night or two? That was fine by him—although he might have to push for a few nights. 'So what did you tell them about your man?'

'I never named him, always kept everything very vague.'

'How long have you been mentioning him?'

'Only in the last couple of months. They've been putting on the pressure for me to visit home and he was my excuse for saying no. Because we've been doing lots of little trips away.'

She didn't want to visit home? 'How long since you've been back?'

She looked away. 'A few years. I've been travelling a lot.'

But there were thousands of planes crossing the globe daily. She could go to New Zealand for a visit and be back the same day. It was obvious there was more she wasn't saying. Did he really want to know what it was?

Actually he was a little curious. But clearly she didn't want to share and he respected her for that. Better than getting a massive 'emo and drama' dump as his ex had always done. But even so, he couldn't let it go completely.

'I still don't really see why you had to make up a whole relationship,' he said. 'And why you want me with you so badly tonight.'

She froze. Carter's radar screamed louder. She was totally hiding something. And he was only human. So he waited, making her reply by pure expectation.

'The truth is I was one of those fat wallflowers as a teen.' Her head bowed as she mumbled.

Carter gritted his teeth to stop his jaw falling open.

'Overweight, acne, rubbish clothes.' She turned away from him. 'Total pizza face. The worst you can imagine.'

Her self-scathing tone rubbed him raw, making him feel an emotion he couldn't quite define. And he couldn't imagine actually. She had the smoothest skin—not a single scar marked her flawless features—and she was so slim—borderline too thin with a tiny waist and tiny wrists and tiny ankles. But she still had some curves that made his blood thicken.

'I wanted to be a whole new me—fit body, jet-set life, great job, gorgeous guy.'

He sighed and reached out to stop those curves escaping from him altogether. So she wanted to look good with a suitable male accessory. He should *not* be flattered about being a good enough accessory for her. That should *not* be pleasing him the sick way it was. But he couldn't help feeling for her. No wonder she was always so beautifully finished—the taunts of teenage years had obviously gone deep. But didn't everyone have scars from those turbulent times? He sure as hell did—it was thanks to the women in his life then that he'd put the Teflon coating on his heart.

'Okay.' He pulled her close and tried to tease her smile

back. 'What do I get out of it? What are you going to offer me?'

Her lashes lifted and the black pools glittered at him. 'You want me so much you'd sell yourself like some sort of escort?'

He was glad to hear her vixen tongue again and he leaned forward to reward her, whispering so close his lips brushed her ear. 'You have to agree that we kiss like nothing else. I'm very interested to see what it'd be like if we did something more.'

'If you wanted something more then why did you walk out so fast last night?' she breathed back.

'Why did you go dance with someone else?'

'That bothered you?' She leaned away and watched his face as he answered.

'I don't do commitment, Penny,' he said honestly. 'But I do do exclusive. And I do respect.'

She drew in a deep breath. 'Ditto.'

He watched her just as close. No sign of the super-quick double blink that happened when she was doing a Pinocchio. Interesting. 'All right, then, I'll come with you tonight, if you agree to stay well away from any other men in the next week.'

'I guess I can handle that,' she said casually. But he could feel her pulse racing.

'You better be sure.' He grinned as her gaze stayed true.

'I'm not promising anything else.'

'We both know that's not necessary,' he drawled. 'It's already a given.'

'This isn't going to get complicated, Carter.'

He really shouldn't feel that as a challenge. Anyway, he thought things were getting that touch more complicated with every passing second.

CHAPTER FIVE

PENNY hadn't seen Matt in just over a year. She'd been in Tokyo then, slowly working her way back to the South Pacific after her years in Europe.

He'd changed—made that final step from boy to man. And he'd almost caught her out in her web of lies. She knew why he was here—it was the start of even less subtle pressure. Her parents' wedding anniversary was coming up soon and they wanted a big celebration—one at home in New Zealand.

She couldn't possibly attend.

She was hoping to save enough money to fly them to her for a holiday. They could afford it themselves of course, but she wanted it to be a gift from her. She wanted that to be enough because she didn't want to have to go to them. The memories were brought to life there in that big house with their ancient, abundant orchard. The wall of trees linked their home to the property next door—Dan's parents' place.

She tried not to think about it and usually, on a day-to-day level, she succeeded. But Matt arriving out of the blue made everything flash in her head movie-montage style. It was almost seven years ago but sometimes felt as recent as yesterday. The darkness of those last few months at home encroached on her vision. And she remembered the estrangement from her family and friends as she'd got mired in a pit of grief and guilt.

She was out of it now. She was strong, she was happy, she was healthy. But the distance from them was still there—literally, emotionally. She didn't think the bridge could ever be rebuilt. In truth, she didn't want it to be.

And in her mind she saw him—as she always did— the day before he'd died. She swiftly blanked the images, focused on pleating the square piece of memo paper she had in front of her. Her fingers neatly folded and creased, working on a displacement activity designed to restore calm.

Because she hadn't coped with what had happened. It had impacted on the whole family and she'd made it worse. Bereavement had shattered the bonds and only by going away had she been able to recover. She needed them to know she was okay. But she couldn't front up to them and prove it in person. Not there. She didn't think she could ever face that place.

Carter couldn't concentrate on the damn transactions. He kept wondering, wanting to know more. In the end he went upstairs and pulled a chair up next to hers. 'We need to work on our story. For dinner tonight.'

She looked completely blank. She hadn't thought this through that far, had she?

He leaned forward and angled for more information. 'So how did we meet? How long have we been dating?'

She turned towards him, her eyes huge. 'I don't know. Can't you make it up?'

'You trust me to do that?'

Beneath her eyes were blue, bruised shadows. 'Sure.'

He stared, on the one hand stupidly gratified, on the other uneasy. What had happened this afternoon to make her look so hurt and exhausted? He glanced at her desk. It was bare, save a folded paper crane—which was unexpected and frankly intriguing.

'Okay, I'll come up with something,' he said, bitten by a random need to reassure her. 'An elaboration on the truth. We met at work.'

She nodded.

'And there was an instant spark.'

She nodded again.

'We were powerless to fight it.'

Her nod was slower that time.

'And we've been inseparable since,' he muttered.

She gazed into his eyes. Hers were so dark he couldn't tell where her pupils ended and her iris began. Black with longing. Right? He leaned closer, feeling unrestrainable longing himself. He wanted to kiss her. Had to. And never stop until she was right back with him. Right here.

Because the sadness in those deep, secretive eyes was unbearable.

He'd seen the attention she got from other men. He wasn't the only one to notice her combination of hotness and vulnerability. She unleashed both passion and protectiveness with just a look. And if they had any idea how she kissed, she'd need a posse of bodyguards to fight them off. Was it just her attention-grabbing trick? He grimaced ruefully; he didn't think so, because she already had him on a three-inch leash.

'Penny with the perfect plait.' He slipped his fingers

into the tight, glossy braid at the back of her head and massaged gently. 'Relax. I'll be the perfect boyfriend. Attentive, caring, funny…'

Why he was saying that he didn't know. He was supposed to be the perfect investigator. He was supposed to be in his office right now working through all the files and finding the point when the discrepancies occurred. Not planning how he was going to spend the evening pretending to be her lover. But she still looked so anxious and he ached to reassure.

'We can laugh and make small talk. Wow the brother and then leave.' He liked the leaving idea. He liked the idea of dressing up with her, going dancing and then dancing some more in private. Yeah, he was a complete fool.

He dropped his hand and stood—a little test of his own strength. 'Are you going to swim first?' He'd learned that was her routine.

She shook her head. 'No time.'

'You want to go home and change?'

'I've got something here,' she mumbled.

'You always have a party-going outfit with you at work?'

She looked surprised he'd even asked.

He went back to his desk for the last hour but all he did was think about her. She was nervous. Why? He didn't think it was because of him—in fact she was relying on him to carry her through this. So why? What was the big deal about her brother? That prickle of protectiveness surged higher. Why hadn't she been back in such a long time? It clearly was a long time. He couldn't wait to go and get some answers.

* * *

Penny stood under the hot jet in the gym shower until the warmth finally seeped into her skin. Over and over she reminded herself that it was going to be okay because Carter was coming and he'd keep it social.

She met him in Reception. He was back in black and another tee that skimmed his hot frame. Pirate Carter. How little she knew about him. How much she wanted to find out.

'You really don't have a girlfriend?'

'Do you think I'd act like this with you if I did?' His expression shut down. 'I don't cheat, Penny. One on one. I expect the same from you.'

She swallowed. 'But this is just for tonight.'

His grin bounced back. 'Oh, sure, you can think that if it'll make you feel better.' He took her hand as they walked along the street, the summer sun still powerful on their backs.

Penny hated public displays of affection. She hated being touched unless she was in a bed and the instigator or lost in the crowd on a dance floor. But Carter ignored all her unsubtle body language. He wouldn't let her pull her hand back, he measured his stride to match hers, drawing her close enough for her shoulder to brush against his arm as they walked. But she tried once more to slip her fingers out of his.

He stopped walking and jerked on her hand so she stumbled near him. His other hand whipped round her waist and his lips caught hers in a very thorough kiss.

She jerked her head back and glared at him. 'What—?'

'If you keep trying to get out of holding my hand, I'm going to keep kissing you. If you want me to act like your boyfriend, I'm going to act like your boyfriend. That includes lots of touching.'

'No, it doesn't,' she hissed.

'I'm an affectionate lover,' he said smoothly. 'I like to touch.'

'Kissing in public is exclusive, rude behaviour.'

'Passionately snogging for hours in front of everyone would be. So you'd better let me hold your hand, then, hadn't you?'

Otherwise he'd passionately snog her for hours? She so shouldn't be tempted by that. 'Don't tease.'

'Why? Did you think I was here to make this easier for you?'

'Of course that's why you're here,' she said completely honestly. 'Be charming, will you?'

'You think I can be charming?'

'You know you can.'

'Why, Penny—' he ran the backs of his fingers down her cheek '—thanks for the compliment.'

'Stop playing with me,' she begged through gritted teeth. 'Please come and talk nicely to him.'

But as they walked closer the cold feeling returned. Until the only warm bit left of her was the hand clasped inside Carter's.

Already seated at the table, Matt watched them approach—correction, he watched Carter.

'Hi, Matt,' Penny said.

Her brother took his steely gaze off Carter and he looked at her. He almost smiled.

An hour or so into the evening, Carter was wondering why she'd been so insistent about his attendance. And why she'd been so anxious. It didn't seem as though her brother was about to bite. If anything he'd looked fiercely protective when he'd greeted them, as if he'd take a piece out of Carter if he made the wrong move. He'd totally given him the 'Big Brother is watching' look. Which was a bit of a laugh, given he had to be the best part of a decade younger. And then he'd started a less than subtle grilling about Carter's background and prospects. Carter had really felt like laughing then, but Matt's questions were astute and intelligent and in less than two minutes he was on his toes and respecting kid brother for that. And he'd gotten no help at all from the woman he was here to socially save. She'd stared intently as he'd answered. She'd probably learnt more facts about him in those minutes than she had in the past couple of days. He'd like to do the same.

So now he willed time to go by triple speed. It refused—in fact he was sure it slowed just to annoy him all the more. Because he wanted to be alone with her. Alone and in his apartment. But there were the mains to be eaten, and more conversation.

'So what do you do, Matt?' Too bad if he should have known already.

'I'm based in Wellington. I've just finished my law degree.'

'So you're going into your first law job?'

'Matt's going to work as a researcher for the judges at the Supreme Court for the year,' Penny interrupted. 'They take three honours grads. Only the best.' Her pride for him glowed.

'I've deferred the law firm job for the year.' Matt shrugged off the accolades.

So he had his future mapped.

'You want to specialize in criminal law?'

'That's right.'

Yeah, that explained the cross-examination he'd just survived. Carter hoped Matt hadn't scoped out the lie right in front of him. Although it wasn't a total lie—Carter did want to be Penny's lover. Just not for ever as 'the man'. He'd settle for just the night. Tonight. Now.

But he forced himself to listen politely as the conversation turned to home and Matt caught her up on the happenings. She was interested, asked a tonne of questions, making him wonder all the more why she hadn't visited in so long. What was so awful about the place when her brother made her laugh about some woman who ran the annual floral festival in their small home town?

'I saw Isabelle the other day.'

It took Carter a moment to register the total silence. The temperature must have dropped too because he could see goose bumps all over Penny's arms again.

'Did you?' she finally answered, her voice more shrill than a rugby coach's whistle. She reached for her water. 'How is she?'

'She's okay.' Matt had stopped eating and was watching her too. 'She's working at the city library.'

Carter had no idea who Isabelle was, but what he did know was that Penny had totally frozen over. Icing over to cover up—what? He tilted his head and looked into her obsidian eyes.

Misery.

Absolute misery.

And she was trying too hard, her smile about to crack. He shot a glance at Matt to see if he'd registered Penny's sudden brittleness.

Yes, he had. He had the same dark eyes as his sister

only now they were even blacker and fiercely focused on her.

She clung on—just—all smile and another polite question. But the façade was as fragile as fine-spun glass. He felt the pressing edge of the knife, waiting for it to slice and shatter.

'You okay?' Her brother ignored her irrelevant question and asked her straight out.

Her lashes lowered and the pretence fell with them. She didn't look at either of them. Carter slung his arm across the back of her chair. She needed a moment of support and that was why he was here. And he wasn't inhuman; his innards twisted at the sight of her.

'Of course,' Penny answered, so brightly it was like staring straight into a garish neon light. 'I'm having dessert. Are you?'

She waved the nearest waiter over and ordered the triple chocolate mousse.

'Excuse me for a moment.' Under cover of the stranger's presence, Matt escaped the underlying tension, shooting a look at Carter as he did.

Penny sat back in her seat after he'd gone and Carter twisted in his to look at her properly. She was even paler now and in her lap her fingers visibly shook. Her mouth parted as if she was working harder to get air into her lungs. Full lips that he knew were soft and that clung to his in a way that made his gut crunch with desire.

She looked terrified. Carter knew there was a big part of this picture that he was missing. But he'd get to that. All that mattered now was bringing her back—bringing back the sparkle, the fight and fire, the gleaming promise that usually filled her.

'Penny?' He slid his arm from the back of her chair to

around her shoulder. Barely any pressure but she turned in to him. Her chin lifted and he saw the stark expression in her eyes.

'You okay?' he muttered as he moved closer. It was pure instinct, the need to protect. To reassure. To make it better.

He couldn't not kiss her.

For a moment she did nothing, as if she was stunned by the touch. But then she kissed him back. Her mouth was so hungry. But then her hunger changed, the tenor of her trembling changed. It wasn't distress any more but need. Her hands clutched his shoulders, pressing him nearer. He wanted to haul her closer still, wanted to curse the fact they were in such a public place.

Her hands tightened round the back of his neck, her fingers curling into his hair. Her breasts pressed against his chest. He wanted to peel her top from her, he wanted to see her as well as feel her. He wanted to touch her all over. He was wearing only a tee shirt and that was too much. He wanted her hands to slide beneath it; he wanted them to slide down his body.

Instead he had to pull back and he had to pull back now.

She didn't move. But her gaze had sharpened, focused. Colour had returned to her cheeks and her lips were redder than they'd been seconds before. She breathed out; he felt the flexing of her shoulders—as if she was shrugging off whatever the burden had been.

Just like that she was back to her perfect image. As if that moment of terror had never happened. As if that shattering kiss hadn't happened.

Carter hadn't felt so rattled in all his life.

There was only one way to deal with it. There was no

going back now. In truth there'd been no going back from the moment he'd laid eyes on her. He'd be her lover for real. He'd see her flushed and on fire and alive. And for someone who'd said kissing in public was rude, exclusive behaviour, she'd been doing pretty well.

Matt noisily returned to his seat and lifted the carafe of water, not meeting Carter's eyes but refilling everyone's glasses as if they all needed cooling down. Carter sure as hell did.

A couple of minutes later Carter was surprised to witness Penny enthusiastically tucking into the chocolate mousse. He'd thought she didn't like chocolate. He thought she worked hard to maintain her figure.

He looked up and saw Matt watching her with wide eyes too. And then Matt looked across at Carter and grinned, the vestige of a wink thrown in. As if he was completely pleased to see his sister putting it away like that.

But because she was so busy dealing with the rich goo, it was down to Carter and Matt to pick up the conversation. Carter darted a suspicious look at Penny. Yeah, she was spinning out the way she was swallowing that stuff—and actually taking the tiniest of forkfuls. In fact he figured she was totally faking her enjoyment of the stuff. Good actress, and calculating minx. But he played along, keeping the conversation safe and saving his questions for later when they were alone.

Only she foiled him.

'Matt can give me a ride home,' she said brightly after Carter had dealt with the bill. 'He wanted to see my flat, remember? And you had to work on those files—you don't want to be too behind tomorrow.'

Carter tried not to bare his teeth as he grinned his way

through acquiescing. He'd been neatly set to the side. But he'd extract a little price of his own.

As Matt went forward to request a taxi Carter pulled her into his arms, so close her body was squashed right up against his. Not as close as he wanted, but it was better than nothing. And as he was staring down the barrel of a night of nothing, he needed a little sweetener. He kissed her, softly, until she opened up for him. Then he slipped his hand up discreetly, quickly rubbing a thumb across her breast. He knew exactly how sensitive she was there. Sure enough he felt her instant spasm, her mouth instinctively parting more on a gasp. But he couldn't take advantage and go deeper. Reluctantly he relinquished his hold on her.

All the wicked thoughts that were tumbling in his head multiplied as he saw her flush and angry sparkle. Yes, it was going to be mind-blowing. But not soon enough.

'Great to meet you, Carter.' Matt walked back from the taxi rank, extending a hand and a bright smile.

So protective little bro wasn't going to throw any punches despite seeing Carter paw his sister? Carter felt smug. He must have the approval, then—on that score at least the night was a success. And he'd claim his reward—tomorrow.

Penny loved her brother but there was only so much she could handle. She yawned and pleaded tiredness. He seemed to understand, getting the taxi to wait while he did a lightning inspection of her flat so he could report back to the parents when he got home.

She stood in her doorway to see him off, thinking she'd got away with the last ten minutes with her nerves intact. Only he turned back, one leg in the taxi already. 'I'm sorry if mentioning Isabelle upset you.'

'Oh, no.' Penny shook her head, swallowing quickly to stop her throat tightening up too much. 'It was so great to see you, Matt. It was a really nice night.'

Aside from that one moment.

'You should come home and visit,' he said, suddenly awkward and emotional. 'You should bring Carter.'

Her throat thickened and tears stung her eyes. Blinking hard, she nodded and stepped back indoors.

Isabelle was Dan's twin and Penny's best friend from age one to seventeen. They'd been closer than sisters. They'd joked about becoming sisters for real when Penny and Dan had gotten together. But then that relationship changed everything—and every other for Penny.

For her, the impact was always there—a weight she carried and could never be relieved of. That was okay, because, as much as she didn't like to think of it, she also never wanted to forget. And her burden was nothing on Isabelle's, or Dan's mother's or his father's.

For so many reasons, Dan's death was the defining moment of her life. The experience and subsequent aftermath were the bases from which she made all her decisions. She wasn't being hurt like that again. More importantly she wasn't hurting anyone else either.

Now she knew life was for living—she would travel, experience and see the world. And always keep her distance.

And that meant distance from Carter too. Especially him.

CHAPTER SIX

'SLEEP well?' Carter stopped by her desk.

'Sure,' Penny lied.

'I didn't either,' he said, eyes twinkling. 'And I blame you for that.'

She didn't rise to his teasing banter. It wasn't entirely because of the memories that had been stirred last night—her instincts had been warning her off Carter from the moment she'd first seen him. She needed to listen to them. He meant danger—not the physical kind, like when she'd thought he was some psycho attacker, but a danger to her head, hormones and heart.

In short, he messed up all her insides.

If she thought she could control it, it would be fine. But she couldn't. Carter wouldn't ever cede dominance and he sought total response. That was fair enough, but it wasn't something she could give.

She wanted to run. That was her usual answer to everything. Only she couldn't. She'd let Mason down if she did and he'd been so good to her and he had troubles enough. He didn't deserve more disloyalty or seeing people flee what could be a sinking ship. If investors got any hint of trouble they might stop the money flow. And

in the current economic climate, that was bad news for
even the most ancient, venerable financial institution.

So she was stuck here for another month or so. And
Carter was only here for a week more. Once he was
gone she'd be okay again. She could be strong and stick
it out—of course she could.

'What, now I've helped you out with your brother
you're ignoring me?' Carter bent and eyeballed her.

'I just think it's better if we keep this on a professional
level.'

'Honey, we've never been professional with each
other.'

'We're adults, Carter. We can try.' To prove the point,
she glanced at him very briefly and offered a tight smile.
Then she went straight back to her computer screen.

'Why do women always have to play games?' He
sighed. 'Blow hot, blow cold.' The amusement in his
voice shouted out his disbelief. 'If I kissed you now,
you'd be ten seconds to yes.'

'I'm not playing, Carter,' she said frostily.

He laughed aloud at that.

But she didn't see him again the rest of the day. She
worked late, ignoring the lump in her throat and the disappointment that he'd taken her at her word. Slowly the
office emptied but she couldn't relax. She really wanted
a swim—alone, which meant after hours. It was the only
way she could think to ease the aches her muscles had
earned from holding her urges in all day.

Jed was on duty tonight so she was in luck. She
grabbed her gym bag from her cupboard. She'd log off
her computer and collect her purse and jacket later; right
now she just wanted to dive into the cool water.

She went via his security station to let him know.

'I shouldn't be that long.' She smiled at the guard. 'Half an hour tops.'

'Sure. I'll lock up in forty, then.'

'Thanks.'

She changed in the small women's room. Kicking the bag under the bench, she took her towel out poolside.

She dived in. The cool water felt fantastic on her hot skin. She stretched out and floated on her back for a while, closing her tired, scratchy eyes. Then she pulled her goggles down and did several lengths. It took longer than usual to get into the rhythm, longer still to try to settle her mind. She was so tired yet she had so much painful energy she didn't quite know what to do with herself—but this wasn't working. Finally she stopped and trod water at the deep end—furthest from the door. Damn it, she'd get dressed and go dancing instead.

She pulled herself up out of the water and turned to reach for her towel. Only someone was there reaching for her instead. Someone who pulled her fast into hot, strong arms. And as she thudded against the wall of masculinity the shrieking fear transformed into sick relief.

'Why do you always have to sneak up on people?' She tried to yell at Carter but it came out like a strangled whisper, her throat all tight with terror.

'Sorry.' His hands smoothed over her shoulders, gently rubbing away her trembles. 'I didn't mean to scare you.' He looked back down at the dim room. 'You're not supposed to be in here.'

'Neither are you,' she snapped. 'Why are you here?'

'Isn't it obvious? I'm looking for you. Why are you here?'

'Isn't it obvious?' She was swimming, for heaven's

sake. She was trying to work him out of her system by exhausting herself.

His grip tightened and he pulled her closer. Her senses were swimming even crazier now. Yeah, the work-him-out hadn't worked.

'You're getting wet.' She put up one last, pathetic defence.

'I don't care.'

'Carter...' she muttered as his mouth descended.

'You don't want me to kiss you?' His lips grazed her temple. 'To touch you? You don't want to touch me?'

Of course she wanted that—she ached to touch him. It was way less than ten seconds to yes.

He laughed, pulling her dripping wet ponytail down the way he liked to, tipping her chin up to meet his mouth. But the laughter died as the kisses deepened and steam rose in its stead.

It was as it had been that first night—a gentle tease to begin with. Until she couldn't resist opening and he immediately went deeper, pushing for more. She lifted her hand and combed her fingers through his silky, thick hair.

His hands slid down her arms, sweeping the droplets from her skin. The hard heat of him burned through his wet shirt. All steel male—with unmistakable purpose.

She managed the first couple of buttons, but he had to do the rest, until she could spread the two halves of cotton and sweep her hands across the hot planes of his chest. Beautiful, hard and hot for her. He saw the look on her face and suddenly tumbled her to the floor, claiming dominance as she'd known he would. The cold tiles were welcome on her burning skin, helping her see straight for one moment of sanity.

'Stop.'

He lifted his head and looked at her.

'You're a player, right, Carter?' she muttered breathlessly. 'This doesn't mean anything.'

He brushed the back of his fingers along her jaw. 'Not if you don't want it to.'

'Just fun.' She rocked, desire making her body move instinctively against his. All she ever had was just a little fun. Nothing more. This had an elemental undertone of something serious that she wanted to eliminate, but the need to have him was beyond necessity now. That big black hole deep inside her had been ripped open and demanded some good feeling to fill it. Like the good feeling she got when kissing Carter.

And then he did kiss her. She closed her eyes as he moved over her—slowly nibbling across her shoulders, his hands working to peel her tight swimsuit down, exposing her breasts. He kissed down her sternum, down to her stomach and then looked back up at what he'd bared. His hands lifted and he cupped her. She shivered at the touch, insanely sensitive there. He rose swiftly, his mouth hot and wide as his tongue swirled around one nipple.

She arched violently, pushing her heels down hard on the cool tiles to get her hips higher—hoping he'd just grip them and surge into her. She wanted it to be powerful and fast. She wanted him to be there now.

But damn him he was slow and toying and touching her all over. His hands slipping into soft parts that she usually held reserved. She tried to guide him back, tried to move her own into dominance—to distract him—but he was focused on his own determined exploration. And it was undoing her completely.

Her whole body broke into a sweat. It was as if she'd

walked into a steam room—suddenly she was so hot, and she couldn't get any of the burning air into her windpipe. She writhed more beneath him, trying to make him move faster—move over her and take her swiftly. She needed it to be finished, because she couldn't cope with heat.

All she wanted was him inside her, riding her, releasing his strength into her. Her mind and body fixated on that one thing—*his* possession, *his* pleasure. Not hers. She got hers from his. That was what she wanted. Not this searing way he was playing with her.

'Carter!' She gasped as his fingers stroked against the strip of her swimsuit between her legs and then slipped beneath the stretchy material. She twisted, suddenly trying to escape him as the strokes grew impossible to bear.

She was drowning, drowning, drowning in the intolerable heat. She couldn't breathe, couldn't think, couldn't control anything. Her fingers dug into his shoulders as the sensations become so strong they scared her.

He lifted his lips from her damp skin. 'Relax.'

How was she supposed to relax? Her toes curled as she flexed every muscle she had, trying to wring the tension from her. But it wouldn't leave her. Instead it worsened.

He sucked her nipple into his mouth and slid a single finger inside. The agony was too complete and she jerked violently—*away* from the source of that frightening intensity. Wrenching herself free from his hold and scooting back on the tiles.

He swore. 'Did I hurt you?' Rising sharply to his knees, his chest heaving, he stared across to where she now sat half a metre away.

She shook her head, breathing hard and shivering as

the sensations still scudded through her. But they were weakening now, becoming manageable.

'Penny?'

'I just needed a second.' Panting, she moved back towards him. Wanting to get the situation under control. She wanted *him* under control. And she knew how—to hold him, kiss him, suck him in deep and squeeze him hard.

Both her mouth and sex were wet with that want. But it was her mouth that wanted first—to lessen his potency. She'd pleasure him enough to make him tolerable for the rest of her, to make him speed up. She wanted him quivering beneath her. She'd be in control again and watch him ride the wave; she wanted to witness the orgasm rippling through him. She wanted to be the source of that pleasure.

Because that was the pleasure in it for her.

Silently Carter watched her crawl back towards him. Still he said nothing as she knelt in front of him. But she felt his ragged breath when she ran her hands down his chest. She spread her palms wide on his thighs, and then she narrowed in on her target. Oh, yes, she loved the size of the erection that greeted her. Her fingers twisted, searching for the zip so she could free him. But all of a sudden he grabbed her hands and stopped her.

She looked up at him. 'Don't you want me to?'

He stared hard into her face—from her mouth to her eyes. 'The setting isn't working for me,' he said. 'We should get out of here.'

She sat back on her heels and swallowed. Suddenly cold. Suddenly aware she was half naked. She wriggled her breasts back into her cold wet swimsuit with absolutely no dignity whatsoever. Not able to look at him again until she was as covered up as she could be, with the towel like a tent around her. By the time she did look across at him he'd fixed his own clothing and was standing waiting for her.

He held out his hand. 'Come on.'

She couldn't refuse his offer of assistance. But as soon as she was on her feet he dropped her hand. He was careful not to walk too close. She was careful not to stare at his strained trousers. She really wished he'd let her do something about that. She really wanted to, wanted *him*, but it had to be her way. Only, as she'd suspected from the first, Carter wasn't one to let that happen.

They got to the door and Carter turned the handle. It didn't move. He twisted it again. Then the other way. It still didn't move.

'It's locked,' Penny said. 'Did you lock it when you came in?'

'No.'

Penny frowned and tried the door herself. Then she looked through the small window to the darkened foyer beyond. 'Jed must have locked it.'

He must have had a quick look in and seen the empty pool—and not seen their entwined bodies in the dark corner at the end of the room. He thought she'd gone so he'd locked it up for the night.

'So we're stuck in here?'

'Looks like it.' She swallowed and drew the damp towel closer around her shoulders.

'We could bang on the door, he'd hear us, right?'

She shook her head. 'He's up one floor and he listens to his iPod.'

Carter rolled his eyes and cursed under his breath.

'Don't make trouble for him,' Penny said quickly. 'I talked him into it. It's my fault really.'

'Why do you come here after hours? Why not when it's open?'

'I like having the pool to myself. It gets really busy before and after work.'

'You don't think it's dangerous?'

'I'm a really strong swimmer. And Jed knows I'm here.'

'He's useless at his job, though, isn't he? He doesn't know I'm in here too.'

'He'd have heard the lift you were in and thought it was me going back up. He probably thinks I left the building while he was down doing the lock-up.'

'Don't try to make excuses for him.'

'He has a young family, he doesn't get much sleep and he needs the job, Carter. Leave him alone.'

'Well, if you really care about him staying in employment then you should stop getting him to break the rules.'

'Okay, fine.'

He sighed and glared back at the deep blue water, and the big still space. Then he looked back at her. 'You can swim in the pool in my apartment complex. It's big and private and hardly anyone swims there.'

'Do you?'

'Yes, but in the morning. You can have it all to yourself at night. And I'll watch.'

'I'm not going to be there at night.'

'Oh, I think you are.' He stepped closer and put his hand on her shoulder. Even through the damp towel she could feel the sizzle. 'You should get dressed.'

She braced for his reaction to this last pearl of info.

'The only way to the changing rooms is through that door.'

'You're kidding,' he snapped, immediately trying the door one more time.

She shook her head.

Carter leaned forward and banged his head on the wood. They couldn't even get to the changing rooms where there might have been a condom machine on the wall. He'd hoped anyway. Because they had no cell phone, no condoms, no couch, no cushions, nothing to cover them in what was going to be a long, cold, frustrating night. He frowned as he felt her shivering beside him.

His clothes were damp and freezing. The whole place was freezing. And all she had on were wet togs and a wet towel. 'What time do they open up in the morning?'

'Six o'clock,' she answered. 'I think the gym attendant gets in around quarter to.'

Just under eight hours away. Eight hours alone with her mostly naked and he couldn't even take advantage of that fact.

'Come on, then, let's try and get comfortable.'

He walked back down to the far end of the pool. Foam flutter boards weren't the softest things in the world, but they were better than cold concrete. He scattered a couple by the wall, gestured for her to take one and he sat on another himself. She cloaked the towel around her and avoided both looking and talking.

Carter tried not to stare at her too obviously while he attempted to work out what had happened when she'd pulled away from him so abruptly. He didn't think he'd hurt her; he'd been being gentle and taking it slow. Well, kind of slow. But it was as if she'd suddenly freaked out—and he'd thought she was so close. She *had* been so close. Right on the brink. Was that the problem? She hadn't wanted to come?

He shook off the idea. So unlikely. Who didn't want to have an orgasm? Maybe he'd touched a too sensitive spot too quickly. Which meant he had to go even more slowly. Which frankly surprised him. It wasn't as if she were some skittish virgin—hell, the way she kissed was so damn hot and welcoming. But when he'd really begun to push for the ultimate? Boom. Was it simply a total withdrawal from a total tease?

Actually he didn't think so. Because her refusal hadn't been total. He didn't think she was playing games—the fact she'd tried to go down on him proved that. But it seemed she didn't want to receive the pleasure herself. Was it some weird control thing? Did she like the power of bringing a man to his knees and begging for her to swallow him whole? Or was she truly that little bit scared?

Wow. She really was a mass of contradictions and complications. And he was beyond intrigued—he was bound to follow through on this with her, he just had to figure out how. His muscles twitched beneath his skin. Patience wasn't one of his virtues. But for Penny Fairburn, he might have to make an exception.

He stretched out his legs and drew in a deep breath to ease the tension still wiring his body. The question now was how to fill in the time. How to tempt her back, how to find out what secrets he needed to unlock her totally. He couldn't make more moves, not in this place, not without warmth, comfort and contraceptive protection. Which left only one thing.

Talk.

'You've always swum?' Lame, but it was a beginning. He couldn't dive straight into all the intense, personal questions that were simmering within him.

'Since I started travelling,' she replied distantly. 'Most places have nice pools somewhere.'

Penny answered his light chat completely uselessly, her brain still barely processing that she was trapped in the pool room all night. With Carter. It was the 'with Carter' bit that really had her reeling. That and the extreme throbbing still going on in some sensitive parts of her body. Staying in control of the next eight hours was going to take serious concentration and she needed to stay in control. The avalanche of sensation he'd triggered in her had taken her by surprise—despite the warning signals she'd had from his earlier kisses.

Too much emotion—even just lust—led to fallout, not fun. She couldn't deal with fallout. Mind you, she might not have to, because he wasn't exactly busting his moves now. In fact he was quite carefully keeping a distance while she grew colder by the second.

He wasn't even looking at her any more. And now the last of the light let in by the high windows was fading so she couldn't hope to read his expression. But he did seem inclined to talk. And she was definitely inclined to ask.

'So your family's in Melbourne.' She'd picked up that nugget at dinner last night.

'Dad is. My mum died when I was fourteen.'

'Oh, I'm sorry.'

'It's okay. Dad's on his third marriage now.'

She clamped her lips to stop her 'oh'.

'He remarried within a year,' Carter continued bluntly.

'Twenty years younger than him, gold-digger. The whole cliché you can imagine, only worse.'

'Oh.' Couldn't stop it that time.

'Eventually he got out of it but went straight into the next marriage. Another much younger woman—Lucinda. They had a baby last year.'

'Really?' That was big.

'Yeah, Nick.'

'You have a baby half-brother,' she processed. 'And you're okay with it?'

'Actually, he's quite a little dude. Why, you don't like kids?'

'It's not that I don't like them…'

He twisted to face her. 'You don't want them?'

'Definitely not,' she answered immediately.

'Not now, or not ever?'

'Ever.'

'Really?' He sounded surprised. 'Me either.' He started to laugh. 'That's what's so great about Nick. He's the new generation Dodds boy to take over from me. No pressure on me to procreate now, Dad's done it.'

'Do you think they'll have more?' Penny couldn't imagine having a sibling she was old enough to be the mother of.

'I don't know. Lucinda probably doesn't want to risk her figure again. She has the new heir now—she has Dad round her little finger as tight as she can.'

'Maybe she loves him.' Penny just had to throw in that possibility because she suspected Carter might have his bitter eyes on.

'She loves his money and status.'

Yeah, bitter. 'Gee, not down on her at all, are you?'

'I've met her type before. The first stepmother—remember?'

'So you're not close to your dad.' She figured his scathing attitude might get in the way of that.

'Actually we are pretty close. He retired from the companies completely a few years ago—mainly to be with her. And part of me hopes their marriage will last because, I think it'd kill him to lose the kid, but it won't. Then he'll undoubtedly find someone else. I try to treat Lucinda with respect. But he knows I don't trust her. He tells me time will take care of that and I guess it will. They'll either break up or last the distance.'

'You don't think it's kind of romantic?'

'I don't believe anything is romantic.'

Ah. Penny sat up and repositioned her towel, her interest totally piqued. 'Who taught you not to?'

Even in the gloom she could see the devilish spark light up his eyes. 'My stepmother's yoga instructor.'

'You're kidding.' She couldn't help but smile. He was so naughty. 'A yoga instructor.' Giggles bubbled then. 'No wonder you won't settle for one woman—she gave you unrealistic expectations.'

'You think she set the bar too high?' he asked, all wickedness.

'A cougar who taught you hot yoga sex? Way too high.' And no wonder he'd shot her through the roof with a mere touch, probably some Tantric trick.

'My stepmother was only eight years older than me,' he pointed out sarcastically. 'And Renee was only six.'

Her name was Renee? Penny maintained her grin, but her teeth gritted. 'But you were how old?'

'Sixteen. What?' His grin broadened. 'Too young?'

'Too young to have your heart broken.'

He laughed. 'That wasn't what happened. It was just sex.'

'Your first time is never just sex,' she said with feeling. 'So what happened?'

'She had a fiancé I didn't know about. She wanted to play around on her man for the power trip. And she wanted to break me in.'

Penny had the distinct impression no woman had ever broken Carter, and none ever would. But he'd definitely been bruised. 'What happens with your first can really leave a mark.' She knew that for a fact.

'You think?' He laughed. 'Renee was just about fun. It was the next one who really tried to do me over.'

'Oh? How old was *she*?'

He chuckled. 'Three months younger than me, honey. She was Head Girl of the school, I was Head Boy. The perfect match—on paper.'

'You were Head Boy?'

He shrugged, looked a bit sheepish. 'Good all-rounder.'

She knew what it took to be appointed the head of one of those elite schools—excellent grades, good sporting or musical achievement, community spirit. The golden boy going with the golden girl. Yeah, she knew all about that. 'So you were King and Queen of the prom. Then what happened?'

'We went to university. She switched to be at the same as me.'

'Oh.' Penny smiled wryly. 'Her first mistake.'

'We were only eighteen, you know? I wasn't looking to settle down.'

She understood that too. And a decade or so later,

Carter still wasn't looking to settle. 'So it turned to custard?'

'She started getting serious about us getting married. Lots of pressure and angst. Eventually she used another guy to try to push me into it.'

'She tried to make you jealous?'

'Yeah, but I don't get jealous. Frankly, I didn't care that much—as bad as that sounds. So it didn't work. I just realised I couldn't trust any of your fair sex.'

He didn't trust women at all. But then who could blame him? His mother had left—okay, she'd died, but it was being left in a sense. His first lover had used him, his first serious girlfriend had tried to manipulate him into something he didn't want…and he'd got ever so slightly bitter.

Well, he didn't need to trust her. He just wanted some fun. In theory he was perfect. Because in theory he posed no threat—he wouldn't ask for anything she didn't want to give.

Except he already had. When he kissed her, his body demanded hers to surrender. Still that step too far for her, but she was so tempted by him she knew she was going to have to figure out a way of working it in a way she could handle.

He was looking at her slyly. 'So what's the deal with your family?'

'What do you mean?' She pulled her legs up tighter and wrapped her arms around her knees. The temperature was really dropping now.

'You haven't been home in years and you take me, a near stranger, to ride shotgun on a dinner with your brother. There's some kind of deal going on.'

'There's no deal,' she said innocently. 'I have a nice family.'

'So what, you're a runaway without a cause?' He looked sceptical. 'There has to be something. Some reason why you don't want to marry or have kids. Not many women don't want that. Most spend half their lives trying to manipulate their way into that situation.'

'You have such a nice impression of women.'

'I call it as I see it. And I like women a lot.'

'You mean you like a lot of women.'

His grin didn't deny it. 'Why limit yourself? And you're the same in that you don't want to settle. Why not? Your parents have an ugly divorce or something?'

'No, they've been married almost thirty years and they're still happy.' Her heart thudded.

'Oh.' Carter looked surprised. 'That's nice.'

'Yeah, they're good together. They're not like you, they fully believe in for-ever happy.'

'So why don't you?'

She fell back on her stock avoidance answer. 'I like my freedom. I like to travel. That's what I do.'

'And you really don't want kids?'

Oh. He'd gone back to that. 'No. I don't want children. Most men who want to marry do. I don't want to disappoint someone. It's easier to be with men who don't want either of those things.'

He looked serious. 'Can you not have kids, Penny?' he asked softly.

'Oh, no,' she said quickly. 'No, it's not that. As far as I'm aware, that's all…fine.' Even in the dim light, she figured her blush was visible. 'I just don't want to bring a kid into this world. It's too cruel.'

He said nothing and eventually she settled back

against the wall, tiredness beginning to pull her down. Age-old tiredness.

'Who's Isabelle?'

'Sorry?' Her tension snapped back.

'You clammed up when Matt mentioned her last night,' Carter said. 'You're clamming up now.'

Penny blew out a strangled breath. 'She's just someone from our home town.' Then she let enough silence pass to point out the obvious—that she wasn't talking any more. She suppressed a shiver and clamped her jaw to stop her teeth chattering. Curled her limbs into an even tighter bunch.

'You're cold.' Carter shuffled closer to where she sat. 'Come on, we have to keep warm.'

That was going to be impossible in this damp fridge. She went more rigid as he came close enough to touch. He sighed and put his arm around her, ignoring her resistance and pulling her down so they were half lying, half propped with their backs against the cold wall.

'Go to sleep,' he said softly, his body gently pressing alongside hers. 'Nothing's going to happen.'

Penny didn't want to wake up, didn't want to move. She was so deliciously warm, even her feet—which were like blocks of ice year round. And a soft wave of even greater warmth was brushing down her arm with gentle regularity.

She wriggled and the warm comfort tightened. The warmth was alive—male arms, bare arms, encircled her. So did bare legs. And against her back? Bare chest.

She jerked up into a sitting position. 'Where are your clothes?'

'You were freezing,' he answered with a lazy stretch.

'So you had to get naked to keep me company?'

'Skin on skin, Penny. It was the best way I could think to warm you up. You wouldn't wake up and I started to think you were getting hypothermic.'

Yeah, right. 'It's the middle of summer.'

'And you're in a basement that's as cold as an icebox,' he pointed out with a total lack of concern. 'You're warmer now, right?'

'Yes.' She was *sizzling*.

'And you're conscious, so it worked.' He pulled her back down to lie against him. 'And you liked it. You burrowed right up against me. You couldn't have got closer.' His arms tightened again. 'No, don't try to wriggle away. I'm feeling cold now. Your turn as caretaker.'

A tremor racked his body, but she could hear his smile. Faker.

She buried her smile in her arm so he couldn't see it. But she didn't try to move away again. Just another five minutes—what harm could that possibly do? He made a fantastic human hot-water bottle.

Then her stomach rumbled.

'You're hungry.'

Then his stomach rumbled too.

'You are too.' She giggled at how loud they gurgled.

'Mmm. We didn't have dinner.' His breath warmed her ear. 'What do you have for breakfast?'

'Fruit, yoghurt and a sprinkle of cinnamon.' Her mouth watered at the thought of it.

'Cinnamon smells good,' he drawled.

'Yeah, so much better than chlorine.' She could feel every inch of him. There were a lot of inches. 'You're in a bad way.' The hard length pressed against the top of her thighs.

'I can live with it.'

'You're sure?'

'Why?' He moved suddenly. 'You offering?'

He rolled above her. She shifted her legs that bit apart to welcome him. Yes, she was offering. Because she knew she couldn't deny herself any more. Desire finally outweighed fear. Some sleep had restored perspective. Besides, given how hard he felt now, she felt confident in her ability to bring him home quickly.

He looked at her closely. She felt his body tense up even more and he smiled, bending forward to close the last inches between them. She closed her eyes, anticipating a full passion blast of a kiss.

Except he merely brushed his lips on her forehead, her cheeks, her nose. So gently, too softly. 'We have the most insane chemistry, Penny.'

She opened her mouth to downplay it.

'No.' He put his fingers across her lips. 'Don't play games. Just be honest. Always be honest with me.'

'Okay.' She could let him have that. 'We have chemistry.' Actually they had more than chemistry. They had some experiences and likes in common. And they also shared no desire for any kind of a relationship.

'And we're going to experiment with it.'

Except there was still that niggling suspicion it might blow up in her face. 'What, like a science project?'

'Pretty much.'

'You weren't kidding about not being romantic.'

'You don't like flowers. You don't like chocolates. You hate romance too,' he teased, pressing even more intimately against her.

'I don't hate diamonds.' She shifted sassily.

He snorted. 'And what would you do if some guy

produced a diamond ring?' He ground his pelvis against hers in a slow circular motion. 'You'd run so fast you'd break the sound barrier.'

She bit her lip to stop her groan of defeat.

'We're going to have an affair,' he told her.

They'd been on this trajectory from the moment they'd laid eyes on each other. All she could do now was try to manage how it went. 'Yes.'

To her surprise the relief hit as she agreed. It was closely followed by excitement. Now she'd admitted it, she wanted it immediately. The sooner she could have, the sooner she could control.

'Tonight.' He levered up and away from her.

She sat up—unconsciously keeping a short distance between them. 'Tonight?'

He grinned at her obvious disappointment. 'No condoms in here.'

Oh. She hadn't thought of that. Thank goodness he had.

'Won't you let me help you out now?' She longed to feel him shaking in her arms. She could stroke him to glory in seconds.

'Will you let me do the same for you?'

She blinked rapidly and ducked his fixed gaze.

'Tonight,' he reiterated, amusement warming his authoritative tone.

She nodded. 'Just a little fun.'

'Can you handle that?' All hint of humour had gone.

Hopefully. If she could stay on top. She looked back into his eyes and waved her independence flag. 'Sure. Can you?'

CHAPTER SEVEN

TWENTY minutes later they heard the door lock click. They hid in the dark corner for another moment and dashed when the coast was clear.

'Get changed quickly,' he whispered.

Giggling in the women's, Penny tossed her skirt and top on straight over her togs, scooped up her bag and was out again in less than a minute. Carter was standing in the little foyer, his shirt water-stained and creased, his jaw dark with stubble. He looked sexier and more dangerous than ever.

He held out his hand. 'Let me take your bag.'

Penny walked quickly. 'I've got it.'

Already people were arriving to use the gym and swim facility and she wanted to get out of there before anyone saw the state she was in.

'No, let me take it,' he insisted, blocking her path.

She frowned but he came even closer, speaking through gritted teeth.

'Look, if you want everyone to see the size of my hard-on, sure, you take it. Otherwise let me just hold it while we get out of here, okay?'

Penny's jaw dropped.

He put a finger under her chin and nudged it closed

again. 'Don't act the innocent. You know exactly what you can do to me. Just like I know what I can do to you.' His gaze imprisoned hers and pierced deep. 'If you'll let me.'

Penny felt as if an adrenalin injection had just been stabbed straight into her heart. The feeling flickered along her veins, molten gold—sweeter than honey yet tart at the same time. Tantalising.

He smiled.

Excitement rippled low in her belly, blocking everything—nerves, memories, fears. All were swallowed in the rising heat. She shook her head but smiled back. Him wanting her felt good. He grabbed her hand and stormed them up the stairs and through Reception.

'Hell, you're not here already, Penny?' Bleary-eyed, Jed looked up from behind his desk.

She shook her head. 'You never saw me.'

'You and I are having a little chat later.' Carter scowled at Jed and held the door for Penny.

He flagged two taxis.

'We can't share?' she asked.

'We get in one of those together now and you know we wouldn't come back. I've got work I have to do.'

Eleven hours later, resentment-filled, she figured he'd done a lot of work. By the time she'd got home, showered, changed and returned to the office, he was already back there and concentrating. He hadn't moved from his chair for hours. She knew because she'd gone into his office a few times—delivering more of the massive numbers of faxes and courier parcels, more wretched files—and he'd ignored her. Hadn't even looked up, lost in a world of figures and transactions and tiny details.

And she hadn't been able to concentrate on a thing—

all jumpy and excited and impatient. Until the tiredness from the little amount of sleep had eaten her nerves and now she was grumpy and ready to stomp home alone because he hadn't even said hello to her all day.

Worst of all, it was only just five o'clock. Theoretically she had another couple of hours to put in first. She glared at her computer screen and banged the buttons on the keyboard.

'So.' He suddenly leant across her desk. 'Your place or mine?'

'So smooth, Carter.' She stabbed through another couple of keystrokes.

'Just answer,' he said roughly, putting his hand over hers. 'I'm barely able to pull together two syllables I'm that strung out.'

She looked at his face and was grateful she was sitting down. No muscles could stay firm against the heat in his eyes. And the grip he had on her now was thrillingly tight. It made her feel a lot better about his distance all day and she dropped any idea of holding out for some grovelling.

'Yours.' She was glad he'd asked. If she went to his it meant she could leave when she needed to, not have to wait for him to decide to go from hers.

'Then let's go.'

'Now?'

The taxi was already waiting and, even better, the trip was short. Her heart drummed faster than a dance-floor anthem and she concentrated on keeping her breathing quiet and even. He still had hold of her hand and as they rode the elevator up to his short-let serviced apartment he finally broke the silence.

'You're tired?'

Actually she was plotting how to handle him. She needed to take charge from the get-go—set the pattern for the evening—and she wanted him on fire as fast as possible.

He must have read her mind because he turned to her the moment he'd closed the door behind them. She melted against him and offered it all, pleased he was so hungry. She wanted him to be uncontrolled, to be in thrall. Passion was powerful and she wanted to succeed in hitting his pleasure high. She moved against him, dancing the way she knew best, her mouth open to his, her fingers working on his buttons—wanting him raw and hot.

But he laughed, low and pure. 'Why are you in such a hurry?'

Because that way she could control it. She shrugged her shoulders and simply smiled, pressing close again.

But he, damn him, suddenly slowed right down. He swept his lips gently across her skin as his fingers so carefully freed buttons. Why was he taking so long to undress her? Hell, they didn't even need to get undressed, he could just push her skirt up and pull her panties to the side—she was ready for him, she would ride hard for him—she badly wanted to feel him come.

Instead his hands drifted south and so did his mouth, gently caressing the skin he'd exposed. Until he was on his knees before her and sliding down the zip of her skirt. She twisted, her discomfort suddenly building, wanting to bring him back up, wanting her hands to be the ones taking the lead. But then his fingers slid higher and she flinched, the pleasure so sharp it was too much, and she couldn't let the sudden rushing feeling swamp her.

Carter had gone completely still. Then he leaned back

and looked up so he could see her face clearly as his hand gently brushed down the front of her thigh. 'I want you to enjoy it.'

'I will enjoy it,' she answered softly. But she knew what he meant. He wanted to hear her scream his name.

He stood, his keen eyes catching the way she wriggled back the tiniest bit from him. He swallowed. 'You don't want me to go down on you?'

She nodded, glad she didn't have to spell it out herself. 'I don't really like that…I…don't feel comfortable.'

He looked thoughtful. 'But you'll go down on me?'

'Oh, yeah, I like that.'

'Well, that's nice.' His devil grin flickered. 'But what turns you on most, Penny?' He watched her steadily.

The heat intensified in her cheeks and she tried to shrug his question off. 'Lots of things…' she mumbled. 'I like…lots of things…'

His head tilted a fraction to the left as he studied her. 'Oh, my…' His arms tightened, his body tensing too as he lanced right through her defences. 'You *fake* it.'

Her mouth opened in horror but the gasp never eventuated. Instead the blush burned all the way down to her toes. She blinked rapidly but she couldn't break away from his all-seeing stare. 'I do enjoy sex,' she said when she got her voice back. 'I like it a lot. It feels good. But… it's…it's just the way I am.'

'You always fake it?' His eyes widened.

'Sometimes it's easier that way.' She licked her lips— not as invitation, but because her mouth had gone Death Valley dry. 'Guys like to feel like they're…'

Carter rubbed his fingers across his forehead.

'It's not going to damage your ego or anything, is it?'

she asked, cringing at his obvious surprise. 'You'd rather
I faked it?'

Blunt as she'd been with him before, this was his kind
of sledgehammer stuff and she was shaking inside. She
was never this honest. But then no one else had ever
called her on it either and she was shocked he'd twigged
at all, let alone so quickly. The fact was, she did fake it.
She had an amazing array of squeals to let the guy think
she was there. The Sally chick who met Harry in that
movie had nothing on her.

But that didn't mean she didn't enjoy it. She did. She
wanted it and she *wanted* Carter. The closeness was
enough for her, feeling desired and making someone
happy even for a few moments made her feel good too.

His gaze hadn't left hers and surprisingly his smile
had gone less devilish, more sweet. 'My ego can handle
you,' he said. 'So no faking. Total honesty. Deal?'

'I want to be with you,' she couldn't help reassuring.
'You turn me on, you know you do. But I just don't…'

'Get across the finish line.'

'But I still enjoy the race.'

He actually laughed. 'Don't feel any pressure to perform for me, darling.' He rested his hands lightly on her
shoulders. 'We can enjoy each other in our own ways.
Let's just see what happens, okay?'

She released the breath that she'd been holding for
ever. 'You're sure?' Even for a guy as confident as him
she was surprised at his easy understanding.

'Yep.' He nodded. 'I'm sure.'

Carter was trying to stop his head spinning but every
thought had just been blown from his brain cells. Wow.
He just hadn't seen that coming and honestly he'd just
blurted the thought that had occurred so randomly.

For him enjoying sex was so inextricably linked with orgasm it was as if she were talking in a foreign language. He tried to figure it out—was she not physically capable of coming?

Actually he didn't believe that. By the pool he'd felt her shaking in his arms, he'd felt the hunger in her mouth, felt the flood of desire between her legs when he'd touched her there. Physically she'd been all systems go.

But at that point she'd literally leapt out of his arms. So it was her head that couldn't let go.

Of course, she was a complete control freak. It made sense. That was her job all over—keeping everything in its place and perfect. But at the same time it didn't make sense. The night he'd met her she'd appeared the absolute image of a hedonist. A beautiful young woman out for fun and frolics and seemingly assured of success should she want it. But it seemed she didn't want it—at least not on a level that she couldn't control. Did she pleasure her lovers rather than let them pleasure her? Because that wasn't right. For him sex was all about mutual delight and exploration. Pleasure for both—give *and* take.

Women didn't have total ownership rights on curiosity. Right now it was eating Carter alive. And so was the challenge. How could it not be a challenge? Because this woman could feel it. He could feel *her*—trembling, all hot and aching. He knew how much she wanted him. So how did he help her let go?

He swallowed again. Like anything it came down to the details. She was so sensitive and maybe it scared her. So he was going to have to take it easy.

She was watching him with a worried look. 'I've probably put you off now.'

And the sweetheart looked as if she utterly regretted that.

He grinned. She didn't need to worry—she would get every ounce of what he had to give. 'Not at all.' Oh, hell, no, now he was all the more desperate to strip her and, oh, so slowly warm her up.

But first what they both needed was a little more time. Just a very little. 'You know we haven't eaten,' he said, tucking his shirt back in. 'Come on, I'll make something.'

She looked surprised.

'You hadn't missed dinner?' Now he thought about it, he was starving.

She shook her head. 'Haven't had a chance to think about it.'

Carter smiled inside again. That was because she'd been thinking about him. The key was to get her to *stop* thinking.

He led the way to the kitchen. 'You don't mind a cold dinner?'

Penny was feeling so hot—from embarrassment—that cold sounded wonderful. In fact she'd dive deep into a pool right now if she could. By the time she'd straightened her clothes Carter was pouring the wine—crisp and cool enough to make condensation form on the glass.

He pointed to the stool on the far side of the bench. 'Sit there and talk to me.'

About what? She'd so killed the moment and she was gutted because she did want to have him. Ugh. She should run away, go dancing and forget everything. 'Are you making any progress with figuring out Mason's problem?'

She was reduced to talking work.

All he did was shrug as he pulled a bowl from the fridge. An assortment of salad greens. He deftly sliced tomato, cucumber, feta and tossed the chunks in, adding a few olives from a tin after. Her mouth watered; she loved a summer salad.

He got a pack from the fridge and forked smoked salmon from it onto plates. Then he got a wooden board and from a brown paper bag slid a loaf of round, artisan bread. Her stomach actually rumbled as he sliced into the loaf. He sent her a wicked look.

'Don't tell me you baked the bread,' she teased to cover it.

'Italian bakery down the road.' He winked. 'Looks good, huh?'

It looked divine. In five minutes he'd fixed the most delicious dinner and she was seriously impressed. 'You always eat this healthily?'

'I work long hours, I'm responsible for a lot of people's jobs. I need to keep fit so I can perform one hundred per cent.'

He picked up both plates. 'Come on, we'll go out onto the balcony. You bring the salad.'

He pushed the bifolding doors wide open. The sun was still high and hot but an aerial sail shaded the table and the view of the harbour was incredible. Pity she was too on edge to be able to enjoy it properly.

'How come it's you helping Mason? Not one of your employees?' From all the conference calls and faxes he'd been getting she knew he didn't usually spend his days on a detailed case analysis like this. He was the boss of more than one entity.

'He trusts me.' Carter lifted his shoulders. 'And he's an old friend. And I wanted a break anyway.'

'So this is a holiday for you?'

'It's a nice little change.'

'But you're still in contact with the Melbourne office all the time.'

He shrugged again. 'I'm responsible for a lot.'

'And you love it.'

'Sure. I like my career. I work hard to succeed.'

Yeah, she'd noticed that about him.

The cool wine refreshed and soothed and now she'd begun to eat she realised just how hungry she was. It was only another five minutes and she'd finished.

He looked at her plate and looked pleased. 'Better?'

'Much.'

He went inside and pushed buttons on the iPod dock in the lounge and then came back to the doorway, offering his hand to her. 'Come on, don't you like dancing?'

'To a much faster beat than this.' But she stood anyway.

He smiled as he drew her closer. 'You've got to learn to relax, Penny.'

The slow jazzy music made the mood sultry and they were barely swaying. His shirt was unbuttoned, so was part of hers, so skin touched. This kind of dancing wasn't freeing, it was torture. She was uncomfortably hot again, her breathing jagged. A half-glass of wine couldn't be blamed for her light-headedness, and she'd just eaten so it wasn't low blood-sugar levels either.

It was him. All him.

And she wanted to feel him wild inside her.

She reached up on tiptoe, deliberately brushing her breasts against his chest. His hand moved instantly to hold her hips tight against his.

She sighed deeply. 'Can we just get on with it?'

'So impatient, Penny.' Laughter warmed his voice. 'Come on.'

He danced her down the little hall to the master bedroom. She liked the anonymity of the room—only one step away from a hotel suite. There was nothing personal of him around to make her wonder beyond what she knew already. Burning out the chemistry was all this was. One week and he'd be gone. Another month and she would too.

He pressed a button and thick, heavy curtains closed, giving the room an even more intimate mood. 'You want the lights out?'

'No.' She smiled. 'I like them on.'

He kicked off his shoes and trousers, shrugging off his shirt. She was spellbound by his body. He caught her looking, sent her an equally hot look back. 'You like to be on top, Penny? You'd like to take the lead?'

She did but she hadn't expected him to let her so easily.

He smiled and kissed her, but then moved onto the bed. He lay, his shoulders propped up against the bed head, his legs long in front of him, and looked back at her in challenge. 'Come and get me, then.'

Oh, she would.

She stripped, her eyes not leaving his as she deliberately, slowly shimmied her way out of every single piece of fabric. His expression was unashamedly hot and he openly hungered as she revealed her breasts.

'You on top works for me,' he muttered hoarsely.

She'd been worried he'd get all serious—forgo his pleasure in the pursuit of hers and then they'd both end up unsatisfied. But it seemed he was happy to stretch back and enjoy everything easily. Thank goodness.

As she walked to the bed he reached out to the bedside table and swiped up a condom, quickly rolling it on. So he was ready. Well, so was she.

She knelt onto the bed, meeting his unwavering gaze, and began to crawl up his body. His smile was so naughty, so challenging, so satisfied.

But she'd see him *really* satisfied. She trailed light fingers up his legs as she moved, bent forward and pressed little kisses, little licks. Nothing but tiny touches designed to torment—his thighs, his hips, his abs, his nipples. She'd get to his erection soon—when he begged.

His breath hissed. 'Are you afraid to kiss me?'

She knelt up and smiled. No. She wasn't afraid of that. She moved up the last few inches and pressed her mouth to his—and felt him smile.

His hands settled on her hips, pulling her to sit on him, his erection only inches from her wet heat. How the man could kiss. Slow and then firm, his lips nipping and then his tongue sliding. He turned it into an art form. He turned it intense.

She shifted, wanting to move right onto him, wanting to tease him some more. But he took her hands in his and imprisoned them beside her hips—so she couldn't touch or move. Then he went right back to kissing her. Just kissing. As if they were young teens on a marathon make-out session.

She was getting desperate now—to touch more, feel more—because his kisses were driving her crazy, building the need inside her. Every one seemed to go deeper. Every one increased her temperature another notch. Every one made her kiss back with the same increasing passion—until it was at an all-new level. She closed her eyes, breathless, yearning for the finish.

Finally he kissed down the side of her neck—just a little. She shivered at the first development of touch.

'Cold?' he murmured against her.

She shook her head a fraction. She was anything but cold.

She was completely naked, so was he, but he didn't move to take her or let her slide down on him. His erection rubbed against the front of her mound, teasing exquisitely.

She wanted to diffuse his power and have him in thrall to her—just for the moments that they'd cling together. That was how she always liked it—to be close, to be held. Intimacy beyond that was too much for her to bear. But Carter didn't seem inclined to settle for anything less than absolute intimacy. Her eyes smarted; she shouldn't have admitted anything to him. She shifted again, eager to move things on more.

'We've got all night, honey,' he muttered between more searing kisses. 'I'm not going to explode if I don't come in the next ten seconds.'

Yeah, but she was afraid she was going to go *insane*—this was too intense.

She rose above him, escaping his grip, demanding they move forward. She glanced down at the broad, flat expanse of his chest and the ridges of his washboard stomach. He was remarkably fit. And before he could stop her she gripped the base of his erection and slid down on him hard and fast.

His abs went even tighter and she felt his quick-drawn breath, but his expression remained calm.

She smiled because he felt so good. So damn good. And she could make him feel even better. She circled, clenching her muscles at the same time, and watched his reaction—the glistening sheen of sweat, the dilation of his eyes. Yes, now she was back in control.

Sort of.

She moved, increasingly faster, increasingly desperate. She searched for that look—the harsh mask of rigid control that tightened a man's expression just before he lost it completely. But Carter stayed relaxed, gazing up at her, his hands trailing up and down the sides of her body, letting her set the pace while still teasing her so lightly.

But the thing was, she was tiring, every time she slid up and down his shaft she felt more sensitised—every stroke hammered at her control. Just looking at him made her senses swim, so feeling him like this had her dizzy. Her breathing fractured. She was unable to keep the swamping sensations at bay, and her head tipped back, her eyes closing. Every inch of her skin felt raw, and at that vulnerable moment Carter slid his hand to her breast.

She gasped, bending forward in an involuntary movement. He caught the back of her head, fingers tangling in her hair, pulling her further forward to meet him. He kissed her again, deep and erotic, while with his other hand his fingers and thumb still circled her screamingly sensitive nipple.

She groaned into his mouth, mostly wanting him to stop—and yet not. And he didn't. Instead he lifted up closer so his body was in a crunch position, his abs pure steel. He wouldn't free her from his kiss, from his caresses, from the powerful thrusts up into her. Slow, regular, his fingers mirrored the rhythm as they moved to scrape right across the tip of her breast. And she wanted to run, she wanted a break—to slow for a second so she could recover some sense.

But the relentless friction of him against her, inside her and the kisses all combined to bring her to a level of sensation she couldn't escape. Devastating. She groaned again, desperate—alarms were ringing but nerves were singing at the same time.

He nibbled on her lips, upping the pressure from every angle, the hand at her breast sliding down hard against her belly to below—to that point just above where their bodies were joined.

She couldn't think any more now. She couldn't move. Too overwhelmed to be able to do anything but be guided by him and that was too much, too scary. But his hands clutched and controlled. He filled her body and all of her senses—all around her, inside her—holding her more tightly than she'd ever been held. And suddenly she realised—she couldn't fall because he'd caught her so close and sure. She was all safe—and free. In the prison of his embrace, she could be free.

And now the heat was delicious. Delirious with it, she danced in the flames—and had no desire to escape any more. For the escape was right here in this moment as she moved with him. Groaning, she sank deeper into the kiss, her body yielding, letting him in that last bit more—she could do nothing except absorb all of him as he relentlessly drove into her.

She was so hot, so incredibly hot and wild and free. It was as if a river had burst inside—a lava flow of sensation and heated bliss. On and on he pushed her along it—intensifying the heat and ride to a point where the waves of fire rushed upon her. Her eyes opened for a second and she broke the seal of the kiss as her breath, heart and mind stopped. There was no scream, no cry, just a catch of breath as her muscles clamped and then violently convulsed.

She shuddered, releasing hard on him with an incoherent moan, her hands clawing, so out of control. She was intensely vulnerable and yet utterly safe in the cocoon he made for her.

She went lax, totally his to mould. And he did, hauling her closer still, his grip even firmer, both hands across her back, pulling her so from top to toe she was flush against his hot damp skin. He frantically ground up for a few more beats and in her mouth their moans sounded like magic.

Reality was on some other planet and she was protected from the harshness of it because she was floating in a pool of paradise set at the perfect temperature.

She'd never been out of her mind before but all her reason had been totally submerged. Now she kept her eyes closed as she glided on that warm tide of completion. Every muscle in her body had gone on strike anyway. She couldn't talk, couldn't open her eyes, would never move again.

He lay a few inches away alongside her, having eased her onto the sheets a while ago. She didn't know how long—time was something she couldn't hope to figure out.

His fingers loosely clasped her wrist and that small connection was just enough. Anything more would be too much, but it seemed he understood that. It seemed he understood a lot.

But he wasn't gloating, wasn't lying on his back and beating his chest like a victorious he-man. And he had every right to do that if he wanted. She wouldn't even mind if he did, she couldn't, because she was so completely relaxed. Actually, she was absolutely exhausted.

But that was okay, because she didn't want to think, to talk, to see. In this moment, she just wanted to be.

Carter really wanted to pull her close, but he suspected she might be feeling super-sensitive right now and he didn't want to overload her system—or freak her out emotionally. Taking it easy was the only way to go. So he fought the instinct to cradle; instead he watched her quietly, waiting for some sign of life. For her conscious reaction.

He already knew her unconscious one. He had his fingers loose on her wrist. He could feel her pulse tripping every bit as fast as his own.

She couldn't fake that.

Sparks of satisfaction fired in his chest and her sudden smile blew them to full-on flames. Because that smile was full of warmth.

'Wow.' Her voice hardly sounded, but he read her lips.

'Yeah.' He couldn't resist—reached out with his spare hand to stroke her hair.

His arms ached even more to hold her. Usually he hated post-coital cuddles—because usually he was too hot and sweaty. And he was damn hot and sweaty now. But he wanted to hold her, to keep the connection open between them. Having her collapse in his arms like that had filled him with the most pure pleasure of his life. He didn't care about his own orgasm after that—only in that instant it had hit and wiped him out.

But now he watched her eyes as the thoughts trickled back into her brain and she was too tired to hide the vulnerability as they darkened.

'I should go.'

He rolled onto his side, towards her, his muscles complaining at the movement. 'I'm only in town for another week. Don't think you're spending a minute of it alone.'

'You didn't say that earlier.' Her dark eyes darkened even more. 'I don't sleep well in a strange bed.'

'You slept okay with me by the pool last night.'

She had nothing to say to that. So he pressed home a point designed to lighten the scene.

'It'll make it easier to be near you at work knowing I'll have you with me all night.'

'Oh, you're back to that argument, are you?' She gave him the smile he'd been seeking.

'Yeah.' He chuckled. 'You'll just have to lie back and think of the company.'

'But I really should—'

'Have you honestly got the energy to get up, get dressed and get out of here right now?' he asked.

Silence for a second, then a very soft answer. 'No.'

'Then shut up and go to sleep.'

Her smile was drowsy and compliant and he switched off the light while he had the advantage. In the darkness he listened as her breathing regulated. He was shattered himself, but he couldn't stop thinking about the experience he'd just barely survived. Yeah, the most challenging moment of his life. He'd been holding back from firing from the moment he'd seen her naked, let alone finally been buried inside her.

She'd been out to claim him—she'd been all tease,

all sensual siren, twisting him hard to force his release, not hers. Now he knew why she liked the light on. She watched him as they moved—noting his reactions and adjusting her movements accordingly. Thinking too much—and all about him. On the one hand she was working out what he liked, and that was great. But not to the extent that she wasn't getting lost in the moment. She was too focused to be feeling it. Like her work, she was determined to be perfect at it. The best. Most guys would lie back and let her, loving it.

And, oh, he had loved it. She'd driven him insane with want for her. But he'd wanted more than that. He'd wanted her to surrender to the exceptional. He'd wanted her to realise and accept this *was* exceptional. And holding back long enough for her to become overwhelmed by their magic had almost broken him. Now he wanted an hour or so to pass quickly so he could recover even a bit of his energy. Because, although he was utterly drained, he couldn't wait to do it all again.

Asleep by the pool last night, she'd curled into his embrace so easily, as if it were the most natural thing in the world. As if it were home. And honestly, he'd enjoyed it. He'd thought that was because they'd both been cold. But he wasn't cold now and he wanted to sleep like that with her in this big, comfortable bed. So he flicked another switch—the air conditioner—cooling the room enough for them to need a light sheet for cover. And for her to want a warm body to curve into.

CHAPTER EIGHT

YAWNING, Penny opened the fridge, her eyes widening when she clocked the contents. 'I wouldn't have picked you to be so into yoghurt.'

'I'm not.' He reached past her for the milk. 'But you said you like it, only I didn't know which sort so I got one of everything.'

He wasn't kidding. There was an entire shelf crammed full of yoghurt cartons.

'I've got cinnamon and there's a ton of fruit in the bowl,' he added. 'Although I got tinned as well, just in case.'

When had he gotten all that exactly? She'd only told him her breakfast choices yesterday by the pool—he must have gotten them in before getting back to work after they'd finally escaped the place. That was efficient. And it deserved a reward.

She leaned closer to where he stood at the bench. 'What do you like for breakfast?'

He swept his arm around her waist and planted a kiss on her smiling mouth. 'You, sunny side up.'

Yeah, she liked that too. She'd woken swaddled in his arms again and the runny honey, so-relaxed-she-could-hardly-stand feeling was still with her. 'You need something more to sustain you.'

'Toast. Eggs. Fruit. Cereal. Breakfast's a big deal for me, especially on the weekend.' His brows pulled together. 'You know I have to work through.'

'I'd figured that already.' She smiled.

'But I have to have your assistance.' Both hands on her waist now, he hoisted her up to sit on the bench.

'Well, Mason did instruct me to do whatever you needed me to do,' she said, giving him a less than demure look from under her lashes.

'Excellent.' His hands wandered more freely. 'Then you're staying right here.'

It was two hours later that Carter sighed and slid out of the bed they'd tumbled back into. 'Come on, we have to go to the office for a few hours.'

Her cherry lips pouted irresistibly.

'I'll get you a coffee from the café on the way,' he said to sweeten the deal.

But it felt like hours later and Carter was sprawled back on the bed still waiting—fully dressed and ready to go. Penny could shower for all eternity, testing his patience even more than when he had sex with her. But then she made up for it by dressing in front of him. She was super quick then and he wouldn't have minded if she'd taken longer...so he avidly watched her every movement. He'd never have guessed that her perfect appearance would take only minutes to achieve. Her well-practised fingers twisted her hair into a plait. He reached across and undid it—earning a filthy look—but it was worth it to watch her weave it again. She had the most beautiful long neck and shoulders.

He drove the rental car he'd picked up at the airport

and ignored 'til now, detouring to her flat on the way so she could pick up some clothes. He insisted on enough for the week and to his immense satisfaction she didn't argue. He glanced round her shoebox while she expertly packed a small case. He looked at the few tiny knick-knacks she'd gathered on her travels. It seemed everything was small enough to fit into a couple of suitcases. Hell, the whole apartment could fit in a suitcase. It didn't surprise him that she lived alone, but he was disappointed not to discover anything much more about her from her few possessions. An ebook reader lay on the arm of the sofa. His fingers itched to flip it open so he could check out the titles she'd loaded.

After he'd stowed her bag in the boot, they stopped at the café just down from the office. He didn't want to take away, gave the excuse that he didn't want to face all those files again just yet, but really he just wanted to relax and hang with her some more. It was peaceful. They split the papers and he skimmed headlines, glancing at her as she concentrated on the articles that really caught her interest—in the international affairs section mostly. He asked and she talked through the list of places she'd lived in. He refused to believe her so she proved it by telling him who was prime minister or president in every one of those countries. Mind you, she could have made a couple of them up and he wouldn't have known. But she spoke bits of a billion languages and was totally animated when she talked about the highlights of each place.

It was almost another two hours and another coffee before they moved on. He picked up the little paper crane she'd made out of the receipt and pocketed it before she noticed.

In the office he had to force himself to pay attention.

But every few minutes his mind slipped to the sensual. He'd woken her through the night, warming her up again. He'd let her set the pace—initially—forcing his patience to extremes so she got so involved there was no pulling back, getting her used to letting go. She was starting to get a little faster already—turning easily into his arms, trusting him with her body. But not quite enough.

He wanted to please her all kinds of ways. He wanted her to trust him to do anything—and for her to enjoy it. She still tried to give more than she took, which was as wonderful as it was difficult. But he was determined to get her to the point of just lying back and letting him make love to her. Of becoming the pure hedonist he knew she could be.

As he had less than a week, he had to go for the intensive approach. Not that he had a problem with that either. He was having a ball thinking hard about ways to tease her into total submission. The trick was taking his time over the stimulation. Not too much, too soon. And maybe he needed to take her where she was at ease the most—on the dance floor or in the water. He liked the water idea. She spent hours in the shower. Uh-huh, he had some serious shower fantasies going.

Back at his apartment that night he cooked a stir-fry as fast as possible so he could focus on her. They hit a bar and club for a while but before long went home and continued their own dance party. She wouldn't let him put the jazz back on, instead she let him in on her favourite radio station—some Czech thing she listened to over the Internet. He'd never have imagined that having sex with Euro-techno blaring in the background would be such an amazing experience.

* * *

Early Sunday, Penny walked with him down to the craft and produce market that burst into being this time each week in the local primary school grounds.

Carter swung the bag. 'Free-range eggs and fresh strawberries—I'm happy.'

She was happy too, but not for those two reasons.

'There are some amazing markets in Melbourne,' he said. 'You ever been there?'

She shook her head.

'You've been to all these other capitals of culture and not Melbourne?' He looked disapproving.

She hadn't gotten there yet and she wouldn't ever live there now. When this week was over she didn't want to see him again. He would become the perfect memory. That was all this could ever be.

To stop suddenly melancholic thoughts sweeping in, she paid more attention to the products on display— organic honey, bespoke tailoring, spices, sausages, pottery, glass, jewellery... She lingered over them, tasting the samples, touching the smoothness of the craftsmanship.

'Perfect for Nick,' Carter called from a couple of stalls away. He waved a bright-coloured, hand-crafted wooden jigsaw puzzle at her. 'Help him learn his numbers.'

'But he's how old?' she teased, walking over to join him.

'Eight months,' Carter answered, unabashed. 'It's never too soon to start working on numbers. He's got to be groomed to take over the business.'

'Thus speaks the accountant.' Had he been groomed from birth too? 'Look.' She pointed out another puzzle that had six circles, the parts cut like pizzas. 'Get him that and he can get to grips with fractions before he's one.' She held it up as if it was the best invention ever.

'Oh, good idea.' Carter took it off her.

'You're not serious.'

Actually it appeared he was.

She shook her head. 'What about this one—this is much more cool.' Like a globe, a fanciful underwater scene with sharks and whales, seahorse, octopus, glitter and fake pearls.

He screwed up his nose. 'Bit girly, isn't it?' Then he shot her a look and winked. 'Okay, that's three.' He gathered them together and then glanced at her, a sheepish smile softening his face to irresistibly boyish. 'Am I going over the top?'

'No.'

'You're right.' Carter reached into his wallet and handed money to the stallholder. 'He's going to love them.'

Penny couldn't help but wonder what Nick looked like—was he a mini-Carter? Did he have his big brother's amazing multi-coloured eyes? She hoped so. She'd love a baby with big blue-green eyes and a cheeky smile. She'd sit her on her knee and pull faces to make her giggle.

Oh, hell, here she was so swamped by warm fuzzies from all the fabulous sex, she was having fantasies about what their babies would look like. She was pathetic.

She never wanted to have children. And Carter most certainly didn't want any.

What he wanted was a week's fling, nothing more. Nor did she. And that was all this was. Okay, so he'd made her feel everything she'd never before felt. But now she'd learned to let go, she would with other lovers, right?

She closed her eyes against the sudden sting of tears and her uncontrollable spasm of revulsion.

She didn't want another man ever to touch her. She only wanted Carter. And she wanted him again now— already addicted to the highs he gave. She felt so good with him. Except that was all this really was—he was the ultimate good-time guy, filled with fun and sun and laughter. He looked carefree in his casual clothes, his red tee shirt as cheerful as his demeanour.

She didn't want him to be so free and easy. It wasn't fair. She wanted him to want her with the same kind of underlying desperation she felt for him. The desperation she was trying to bury deep and deny.

But she had the compelling urge to push him into a glorious loss of control. Because even though she knew they shared the most amazing sex, it was she who lost it first. He always hung on until she was truly satisfied. And while he was the only lover ever to have been able to do that for her, part of her didn't like it. It made her feel like the weaker link. She knew that didn't really matter—this wasn't going past the one week. She wished she could shatter him just once.

But she was the one falling apart.

She tugged on his hand and turned to face him. 'Kiss me.'

Carter looked at her. He could feel the tremors running under her skin. What had happened in the last sixty seconds to make her so edgy?

'I thought you didn't like lust in public?' he teased to joke a smile out of her.

'Just kiss me,' she said.

And how could any man resist a sultry command like that? Carter pulled hard on her hair so her head tilted back. He kissed down the column of her exposed throat. With his other hand he pushed her pelvis, grinding it into his.

He stepped back pulling her into the shadows behind a row of stalls. Truthfully he didn't do public displays much—and certainly not of unbridled lust like this. But the moment he touched her he was lost. Uncaring about what anyone thought, he just had to hold her closer and let the glory wash through him.

'You are amazing.' Breathing hard and deep, she looked at him, her black eyes shining. Suddenly she smiled. 'You make me feel so good.'

His skin prickled. Okay, that was nice because he did aim to please, but it wasn't just the kissing that made him feel good. Fact was, he felt good every moment he spent with her.

After the market it was back to the office for a long afternoon that Penny struggled through every second of. Baby images kept popping in her head. Cute Carter-as-a-kid imaginings. So stupid.

When they finally returned to his apartment he went fussing in the kitchen, so Penny swam in the pool—needing twenty minutes alone to sort out her head. But a zillion lengths didn't really help so she went back upstairs. Something smelt good and Carter was busy on his computer. She didn't think he even noticed when she walked past on her way to shower. So much for the revitalising benefits of exercise—all she felt was even more tired and emotional. She wanted to fall into his arms again and let him take her to paradise. She wanted him to hold her and never let go.

It was the sex. Her weak woman's body wanted to

wrap around his and absorb his strength. But he was mentally miles away in an office in Melbourne controlling his companies. So she could control merely herself, couldn't she? She flicked on the lights in the big bathroom and twisted the shower on. She stood under the streaming jet and let the water pummel the tension in her shoulders.

'Is it okay if I join you?' His erection pointed to the sky, already condom sheathed.

Her bones dissolved, she leant against the wall, wanting to cling to him and just hang on for the ride. His face lit up, his low laugh rumbled and he flashed a victorious smile.

She closed her eyes because his all-male beauty was too much to witness. But when she opened them again, everything was still black. The room was totally dark.

'Carter?' she asked quickly. 'What happened?'

'Bulb must have blown.' He stepped into the wet space with her.

She slid her palms all over his chest, loving it as the water made him slick. It was like discovering him all over again only by touch this time, not sight. Somehow it seemed more intimate, more intense. He pulled her close and kissed her. Oh, she loved those kisses. She loved the way he twisted her hair into a rope and wound it against his wrist—pulling it back, exposing her throat to his hot mouth. And then he went lower.

She gasped and pressed back against the cool wet tiles as he licked down her torso. His hands cupped her breasts, lifting them first to the water, and then to his tongue. She shuddered, the sensations excruciatingly sublime.

In the velvety darkness all she could do was soak up

his caresses and listen to the falling water. As he gently, rhythmically tugged on each nipple with his lips, her knees gave out. He grasped her waist, easing her to the floor and following, kept doing those, oh, so wickedly delicious things with his tongue and hands.

Blind to everything but sensation, she groaned and his kisses went even lower. She reached, finding his broad shoulders with her hands and sweeping across them, loving the smooth hot skin and the hot water raining on them.

She arched up, unable to stop her response to the wide, wet touches, hardly aware of who she was any more. His hand splayed on her lower back, pushing her closer to his hungry mouth. The other he used to test her, torment her, tease her. Just one finger at first, smoothly entering her slick heat. She gasped, but his tongue kept stroking, and then she was blind to everything except how it felt. She moved uncontrollably, rocking to meet him. Panting, she shuddered as he plunged deeper, and withdrew only to return with more. She was so sensitive to the way he toyed with her, and in the dark, wet heat all she could do was *feel*. Her fingers, thighs, sex pulsed and gripped as all she felt was pure lightning-bright pleasure. The orgasm knifed through her—ripping her to exquisitely satisfied shreds. She totally lost her mind.

His muscles bunched and rippled beneath her clutching hands. Displaying a scary kind of strength, he scooped her up again and flattened her against the wet wall. His hands cupped her, spreading her so he could thrust straight in. She wound her legs around his waist and had no hope of controlling anything. Not her instinctive rhythm, her screams, her next orgasm. Not when he held her and kissed her and claimed her so completely.

The water ran down them as they leaned together, taking for ever for their breath to ease.

'Are you okay?' he finally spoke. 'That wasn't too uncomfortable?'

She mock-punched his arm. 'Carter.'

He started to laugh. And then she laughed too.

'You sure you didn't mind?' His laugh became a groan as he carefully curved his hands around her hips.

How could she mind that? 'Give me half an hour and then do it again, will you?'

'You don't need half an hour.' He swung her into his arms and carried her back to his bed. And made love to every inch of her all over again.

Monday morning she couldn't move. Wouldn't. Point blank refused to let the weekend be over. She screwed her eyes shut when he appeared by the bed dressed in one of his killer suits. 'Don't ask me to get up yet. Please.'

She just wanted to snuggle in the sheets and enjoy absolute physical abandonment. He was perfect. He was playful. He wasn't ever going to ask anything more of her. And now he was fresh from the shower.

All she could let herself think about was this. She buried herself in his sensuality, blinding herself to everything else that was so attractive about him. Ignoring the ways in which they were so compatible.

But the humour she couldn't avoid—not when he brought it into bed with them.

He tugged the sheet from her body; she stretched and squealed with the pleasure-pain of well-worn muscles. She really didn't want to get up yet. But then he unzipped his trousers. Delighted, she scrunched a little deeper into the mattress.

'Oh, my,' she murmured as he straddled her. 'You want me to set a personal record or something?'

'Well, it's like anything—the more practice you have, the better you get.'

'Then hurry up and practise with me.' Oh, she was so into it now—utterly free in the physical play with him.

His brows lifted.

'Come on,' she begged. 'You'll have me hit orgasm just from thinking about it soon.' Just from thinking about *him*.

'You're complaining?'

'No,' she giggled as he nuzzled down her stomach like a playful lion.

Suddenly he stopped and looked up her body into her eyes. 'Seriously, though, you're not too sore?'

She arched, brazenly lifting her hips to him. 'Don't you dare stop!'

Monday sucked. Monday meant other people were in the office—meaning he couldn't go and kiss her freely. So Carter locked himself in his office and ploughed on with the tedious task of hunting for tiny financial irregularities. He didn't move from his desk for hours—just to prove to himself that he could concentrate for that long. Because all he really wanted to do was hang out by Penny's desk and talk to her. He wanted to spend every minute with her, resenting the job he had to do, even though it was because of the job that he'd met her in the first place.

Tuesday sucked just as much—another night had gone and the ones remaining felt too few. Stupid. Because he'd achieved his aim—she was wholly his and he had the rest of the week to indulge and that should totally be enough.

And now he'd just found the needle in the haystack. He carefully pulled it out to inspect it—drawing with it the thread that could unravel the whole company. Once he'd followed the poison all the way to the source, and gathered the documentation, his job was done.

Success all round.

He could go back to his own business, in another city, and get on with it. So he didn't need to feel this rubbish.

Wednesday he was even more grumpy, the evidence was almost complete, but Penny was out and he wanted her to hurry up and get back so they could go to lunch. He went up to her office to see if she was back. There was someone there, but it wasn't Penny. It was her brother.

'Hi, Matt.' Carter held out his hand. 'Penny's not here. She's taken some stuff to Mason. She shouldn't be more than another half-hour.'

'Oh.' The younger man shifted on his feet. 'I can't wait. I have to get to the airport.'

'She'll be sorry she missed you.' Man, her family was awful at communication. This past fortnight he'd been away, Carter and his dad had Skyped a couple of times, and he'd been sent the latest picture of Nick looking cute. There were no excuses in the technology age. But Matt looked so disappointed, Carter felt bad for him. 'I'll walk out with you.' He led him back to the lift. 'Conference was good?'

'Yeah.' Matt smiled but looked distracted.

'You want a taxi called?' Carter blinked as they got out in the broad sunshine.

Matt didn't answer, still looked both disappointed

and distracted. 'You'll take care of her, won't you?' he suddenly said. 'She needs lots of support. She's been cut off for so long.'

Yeah, that was pretty obvious. Carter waited. Because Matt looked as if he had something on his mind he wanted to share. And it didn't look like happy thoughts.

'She hasn't been back home since she went away. Not once. That's seven years.' Matt stared across the street. 'Mum and Dad are desperate for her to. Maybe she'd come with you.'

'I'll talk to her about it.' That and a few other things. Carter wanted to know so much more. Like everything.

'I know I shouldn't have mentioned Isabelle. But I wanted to see what would happen.'

Carter knew he was in murky waters without any floatation device, so he just nodded and waited. Fortunately Matt soon filled the gap.

'I saw you taking care of that.'

Carter faked a small smile. He supposed kissing her was one way of taking care. Pretty basic but it had been effective at the time.

'I didn't think she was ever going to get over Dan and get that close to another guy,' Matt continued. 'When she started mentioning you in emails I couldn't believe it. For a while I thought she might have been making you up. But you're real. And I can see how it is between you.'

Carter's brain processed even faster than its usual warp-factor speed. Dan? Who the hell was Dan? Hadn't they been talking about someone called Isabelle?

'She looks better. She looks fitter than she did when I saw her in Tokyo last year,' Matt added. 'You're obviously good for her.'

Anger flared in Carter's chest. What did it matter if she looked fit? Maybe this was why she didn't want to see her family—were they too obsessed with a perfect image? Who cared if she put on a few extra pounds or didn't swim her lengths so religiously? He sure as hell didn't. He just liked her laughing. So he answered roughly. 'She likes my cooking.'

'After he died she never used to eat with us.' Matt shook his head. 'Those last months it was like she wasn't there. She didn't want to be. She got so skinny you could see every vertebra in her spine. Every rib. Every bloody bone.'

The bottom fell out of Carter's world completely. He couldn't speak at all now. He stared at Matt, replaying the words, reading the tension etched on the younger guy's face.

'But she seems really happy now.' Matt cleared his throat and kept staring hard at some building over the road. 'I want her to stay that way.'

Was that why Matt had looked so pleased to see her eating that chocolate mousse? Because Penny had once been so sad she'd starved herself sick? Tension tightened every muscle. Carter folded his arms across his chest to hide his fists.

'She's not going to move again, is she? She's settled, with you, right?'

Carter's brain was still rushing and he didn't know how he could possibly reply to that.

'Because it's coming up to moving time for her but she's not going to now, right?' Matt turned sharply to look at him.

Carter put his hand on Matt's shoulder—to shut him

up as much as anything. 'Don't worry.' He avoided answering the question directly. 'I'll take care of her.'

'Yeah,' Matt croaked. 'Thanks for caring about her.'

Matt was avoiding his eyes again now and Carter was glad because he wouldn't have been able to hide his total confusion.

'I better get going.'

Carter fumbled in his pocket and pulled out a business card. 'Stay in touch.'

Matt handed him his too. Carter pocketed it and got back into the building as fast as he could. Then he took the stairs—slowly.

Dan. Who the hell was Dan?

Some guy who had died. And Matt hadn't thought Penny would get close to another guy again. Penny, who hadn't been home since…

Seven years ago she'd have been seventeen or eighteen. It didn't take much to work it out. While he'd yet to figure Isabelle's place in the picture, the essentials were obvious.

Dan must have been Penny's first love—and hadn't she once said the first left a real mark? That it was never just sex? Carter felt sick, hated thinking that Penny had suffered something bad.

He'd never felt that kind of heartbreak. He'd been betrayed—but that had meant more burnt pride than a seriously minced-up heart. And since then he hadn't let another woman close enough to inflict any serious damage. But to love someone so deeply and lose them, especially at such a young age? Yeah, that changed people. That really hurt people.

And weirdly, right now, Carter felt hurt she'd held back

that information from him. Which was dumb, because it wasn't as if they'd set out for anything more meaningful than some fun.

But he knew how bereavement could affect people. Hadn't he seen it in his dad? His parents had been soul mates, so happy until the cancer stole his mum away decades too soon. And his father hadn't coped—couldn't bear to be alone—walking from one wrong relationship to the next. Searching, searching, searching for the same bliss. And every time failing because nothing could live up to that ideal.

For the first time he felt a modicum of sympathy for his father's subsequent wives. Imagine always knowing they came in second. They could never compete with that golden memory. But Lucinda was trying, wasn't she? Giving Carter's dad the one thing he'd wanted so badly— more family. And sticking with him now for years longer than Carter had ever thought she would—providing the sense of home and security that had been gone so long. Carter's respect for her proliferated just like that.

Then his attention lurched back to Penny. Questions just kept coming faster and faster, falling over themselves and piling into a heap of confusion in his head. He wanted to know everything. He wanted to understand it all.

But he didn't want to have to ask her—to hear her prevaricate, or dismiss, or, worse, lie. He wanted her to tell him the truth. He wanted her to trust him enough to do that. The hurt feeling in his chest deepened. Somehow he didn't think that was going to happen in a hurry.

He knew it was wrong. But he was a details man and he'd get as many as he could, however he could, because he was low on advantage points. In the office he opened the filing cabinet and pulled her personnel file. Her being a temp, there wasn't much—just a copy of her CV, security clearance and the references from the agency. Brilliant ones. But it was the CV that he focused on. The list of jobs was almost a mile long. And so were the towns. She'd been serious about her travelling. She'd moved at almost exactly the same time each year. Britain, Spain, Czech Republic, Greece, Japan, Australia.

The regularity with which she'd moved made his blood run cold. Never more than a year in the one town. He looked on the front of the file that recorded the date she'd started at Nicholls—seven months already. But she'd worked at another temp job in the city for four months before that. So her year in Sydney was almost up. When that time ticked over would she move to another place? If so, where? There seemed to be no pattern to the destinations. She just moved, running away—from something big.

Had her heart been that broken? His own thudded painfully because there was someone in her past whose death had cut her up so badly. Who'd put her off relationships—so far for life. She acted as if she wanted fun but she could hardly let herself have it—not really. She wasn't the brazen huntress he'd first thought. Not selfish or self-centred. Certainly not any kind of free spirit. She worked conscientiously—and she cared. She was a generous giver who struggled to accept the same when it was offered in return. And hadn't he seen it those few times—the vulnerability and loneliness in her eyes?

She was hiding from something even she couldn't admit to.

He flicked through the CV again and another little fact caught him. She'd been Head Girl at her school? He half laughed. No wonder she'd been interested when he'd mentioned he was Head Boy. And she'd said nothing, secretive wench. He looked closer. Her grades were stellar. Really stellar. He frowned—why hadn't she gone to university? She would have had her pick of colleges and courses with grades like those. But she'd gone overseas as soon as school had finished and she hadn't been back. She must have been devastated. And for all the party-girl, clubbing life she lived now, she obviously still was.

His upset deepened. He hated that she covered up so much. He liked her. He wanted to know she was okay. He wanted to be her friend. He actually wanted *more*.

Well. That was new.

He'd never met a woman who held back her emotions the way she did. Okay, he'd freed her from one aspect of that control. Maybe he could cut her loose from another? Even if he suspected it was going to hurt him to try. Could he bear to know the extent to which she'd loved that guy?

Pathetic as it was, he was jealous. She'd cared so much for Dan she'd been devastated. Carter wanted her to care about him instead.

But how could he ever compete with the perfect first love? He winced even as he thought that thought. He didn't have to. He didn't want her so totally like that— did he? Did he really want to be the one and only, the number one man in her life?

No. Surely not.

But in a scarily short amount of time she'd become important to him. Her happiness had become important to him. And he wanted her to trust him enough to talk. Sure she'd opened up sexually—but it was the only way she'd opened up. And in some ways it was another shield in itself. Just a fling—it was the defence he'd used for years himself, even with Penny to begin with. And hadn't it turned around to bite him now? He'd never been in a situation so confusing, so complicated. An adulterous older woman and a manipulative girlfriend seeking an engagement ring had nothing on Penny and her inability to share. Hell, she must have such fear.

His anger deepened because he wanted her to be over it and feel free to fall in love again. Preferably with him.

In the evening at his apartment she was the same smiling flirt, teasing him, talking it up—the banter that, while fun, didn't go deep. He had to bite the inside of his lips, bursting inside to ask her what had happened. Desperate to know where her heart was at now. But he wanted her to offer it, not to have to force it.

She let him lie between her legs, all warm and impishly malleable, smiling at him delightfully. It wasn't enough.

He kissed her tenderly. As if she were one of the fragile flowers she said she didn't like.

'Don't.' She frowned and swept her hands across his back. He knew she was trying to hurry him.

'Don't what?'

'Be so nice.'

He carefully studied her. 'You think you don't deserve someone being nice to you?'

She just closed her eyes.

And then he didn't even pretend to let her take the lead. He dominated. Intensely focused on making love to her. It was about more than just giving her pleasure, but about bringing her closer to him any way he could.

Afterwards he lay holding her sealed to him, refusing

to let her wriggle even an inch away, telling her more about his work in Melbourne. Stupid stories about his youth. Trying to grow the connection between them. To build trust. Blindly hoping she might talk back.

But all she did was listen.

CHAPTER NINE

CARTER took a taxi to Mason. He had the files; the job was done. In theory, after this meeting, he was free to fly out. But he couldn't bring himself to book a ticket.

The old man had aged more in the last week than he had in the last ten years. Guilt squeezed Carter—he should have been to see him sooner. But Penny had been making daily visits with paperwork and sundry items. Even so.

'I've got the information you need.' He dragged out a smile and put the small packet of printouts on the dining table. 'It's all there. Once spotted, the pattern is pretty obvious.'

'I knew I could rely on you.' Mason sank heavily into his favourite chair.

'Get in your auditors. It won't take much to sort it out.'

'He'll have to be prosecuted.'

'Yes.' Carter nodded. 'But I think the impact will be minimal because we caught him.' He tried to put the best spin on it. 'And quickly too. If anything the investors should be impressed at the efficiency of your system checks.'

'It was instinct, Carter.' Mason shook his head. 'Just a feeling.'

'Well, you've always had good instincts, Mason.'

'And now my instinct is telling me I've failed.'

'In what way?' Surprised, Carter nearly spilt the coffee he was pouring.

'That company is my life.' Mason stared past him to the big painting on the wall. 'And in the current climate it could have been swept away so quickly if this had got out of hand. It makes me wonder what's going to be left after I'm gone. It'll probably be bought out, the name will go. It'll be finished.'

Carter inhaled deeply. Mason had long been his mentor. He'd admired the dedication, the drive, the single-minded chase for success. And there had been huge success. 'You've already built an amazing legacy, Mason.'

Mason lifted his arms. 'What is there? A house? A few paintings that will be auctioned off? Where are the memories? Where's the warmth?'

The unease in Carter's chest grew. Mason's wife had died early on in their marriage—before they'd had time to have kids. And Mason had buried his heart alongside her. As far as Carter was aware there hadn't been another woman—totally unlike his father. Until now Carter had always respected Mason more for that. But now he wasn't so sure—not when he was confronted with Mason's obvious regrets. And loneliness. Another lonely person. 'You've given so much to charity, Mason. You've helped so many people.'

'Who have their own lives and families.' Mason sighed. 'I shouldn't have been such a coward. I should have tried to meet someone else. But I just worked instead.'

'And you've done great work. You've employed lots of people, you helped lots of people.' That was a massive achievement.

But personally fulfilling? Yes and no.

'How's Nick?' Mason asked.

Carter's grin flashed before he even thought. 'He's a little dude.'

'Your father is a braver man than me. I regret not having a family. I regret devoting all my life to accumulating paper.'

'Hey.' Carter leaned forward and put his hand on Mason's arm. 'You have me.'

Mason said nothing for a bit, just stirred the milk in his coffee. Then he set the teaspoon to the side. 'Is everything else at the office okay?'

'Penny has it all under control.'

'Told you she was an angel.'

Carter winced through a deep sip of the burning-hot coffee. 'Yeah.'

A broken angel.

He sat back in his chair and settled in for the afternoon. He'd hang with Mason. He needed the time out to think.

Penny had been desperate for Carter to return from Mason's—he'd gone to hand over what tricks he'd found but he'd been gone for hours and, being a complete Carter addict, she was antsy with unfulfilled need. Resenting the waste of the precious few minutes she had left. Finally he showed up, just as she was about to pack up and go to her own flat and cry.

So she went to his apartment instead. She had no shame, no thought of saying no. They only had a night or two left, and she wanted every possible moment with him. Because she wasn't thinking of anything beyond the present moment. She couldn't let herself.

He was unusually quiet as they walked into the apartment building. Maybe it hadn't gone well.

'Was Mason okay?' She finally broke the silence.

His shoulders jerked dismissively. 'Pleased with getting the result.'

Okay. He didn't just look moody, he sounded it too. Once inside, he tossed the key on the table and turned to look at her.

Wow. She walked over to him—obeying the summons. She tiptoed up and kissed his jaw. Did he want her to take the lead this time?

It seemed so. She kissed him full on the mouth— teasing his lips with her teeth and tongue. His eyes closed and she heard his tortured groan. It thrilled her—maybe this was her chance to make him shatter. Was he tired and needy and impatient? The thought excited her completely because she ached for him to want her so badly he lost all his finesse. Quickly she fought to free him from his clothes. Oh, yes, he wanted her—she could feel the heat burning through him. But his hands lifted and caught hers, stopping her from stroking him.

'Matt called by the office yesterday.' He all but shouted in her ear.

She pulled back to look at him. 'He did?'

'Passing by on his way to the airport.'

'Oh.' She was sorry she'd missed him. She had to do better at staying in touch. She'd text him later.

'We had a little chat.'

'Did you?' Little goose bumps rose on her skin—because Carter's expression had gone scarily stony.

'He said you're looking better than when he saw you in Tokyo. And way better than you did years ago.'

She blanched at the bitter tone in his voice.

'You've put weight on, Penny. Not taken it off.'

'Oh, don't, Carter.' She turned away from him.

'What, speak the truth?' He laughed roughly. 'Penny, what on earth is going on?'

'Nothing.'

'You lied to me. You said you were overweight as a teenager. But you weren't, you were a walking skeleton.'

'Does this really matter?'

'Yes, it does.'

'Why?'

'You've been using me this whole time to get off. To hide from whatever nightmares it is that you have.'

And what was so wrong with that? It wasn't as if he'd been offering anything more. 'I thought the whole point of this was for us to get off.'

'Yeah, well, if it's only orgasms you want, Penny, get yourself a vibrator.'

Oh, that made her mad. She turned back, found him less than an inch away—so ran her hand down his chest.

He jerked back. 'I'm not interested in being your sex toy.'

'Really?' She reached forward and cupped his erection. 'Maybe you'd better tell your penis that.'

'I can control it.' He stepped away. 'If you want to get off, why not go find someone else? Any of those analysts in the office will stand for you. Hell, you could have all of them at once if you want.'

She flinched. She didn't want another lover. None. Ever.

'I'm not interested in being your man whore,' he snarled. 'I actually have more self-respect than that.'

'What are you interested in, then?' she said, stung to anger by his sudden rejection. 'You were the one looking at me like that.'

'Like what?'

'You know what,' she snapped. 'All simmering sex.'

He just laughed—bitterly.

That pissed her off even more. She pushed back into his space. 'You were stripping me with your eyes and you know it.'

'And you were loving it.'

'So what the hell do you want?' Why was he going septic on her when they wanted the same thing?

'I want the *real* thing—if you even know what that is. Because maybe you've been faking all along? You said yourself you usually do. How would I know? You're so damn good at lying and holding back.'

She gaped for a stunned second. 'You think I was faking?' Now she was furious. And really hurt. She'd never felt like that with anyone, never let anyone…not like that.

He filled the room, his arms crossed, watching her with that wide bright gaze that revealed nothing but seemed to be searching through all her internal baggage.

'I *wasn't* faking.' Jerk. As if that kind of reaction happened every other day? She wouldn't have practically moved in with him and be making an idiot of herself lying back and letting him do anything, if she didn't feel as if it were something out of this world. And she wouldn't be so completely miserable about it being the end of the week if she hadn't been more than moved by him—in so many more ways than sexual. And she really didn't want to be getting upset about it this instant. But her eyes were stinging. Angrily she tried to push past him.

But his arms became iron bars that caught and brought her close against his body. 'I know you weren't.' He sighed. 'I'm sorry.'

'What is your problem?' she mumbled, completely confused now.

His hands smoothed down her back. His hardness softened her.

'I want to know where I stand with you,' he said. The gentle words stirred her hair.

'What do you mean?' She tilted her head back to read his expression and swallowed to settle her tense nerves. 'There's nowhere to stand. We're having a fling.'

'Not enough.'

Her heart thudded—beating caution now, rather than anger.

His gaze unwavering, he told her. 'I want more.'

How more? What more? Anything more was impossible. Tomorrow was Friday. They were almost at farewell point.

As his gaze locked hers the safe feeling she'd had all week started to slip. Why was he messing with the boundaries?

'You're leaving here…' Her breathing shortened. 'Like on Saturday. This was just for—'

'Fun,' he finished for her. 'Yeah, roger that. But we can still be friends, can't we?'

Friends? She didn't have that many of those. Plenty of acquaintances. But not very many friends. And what did friends mean—did he want this to go beyond the week? Because she couldn't do that—she had to keep this sealed in its short space of time. She *had* to keep those emotions sealed. She tried to step back but his hands tightened. She broke eye contact. 'I don't think we need to complicate this, Carter.'

'Talking won't make it complicated.'

He wanted to talk? About what?

'Can't you let me into your life just a little bit, Penny?'

'Will you put some clothes back on?' She couldn't think with him like this.

'Why?' he answered coolly. 'I'm not afraid to get naked with you, Penny. I'm willing to bare all.'

'Don't be ridiculous, Carter. This is a one-week fling.' She pushed away from him—and he let her. 'You don't want to talk any more than I do. Why waste that precious time?'

'When we could be rooting like rabbits?'

'You like it that way. It's what you've wanted from me from the moment we met.' She turned on him, hiding her fear with aggression. 'You're not interested in me opening up to you in any way other than physical.'

'Not true.'

'Totally true. As far are you're concerned all women are manipulative, conniving cows who're trying to trap men into marriage.'

'Many of the women I've met are.'

'Well, I'm not like them.'

'And that's one thing we will agree on.'

She blinked. Then shook her head. This conversation was going surreal. Why was her ultimate playboy going serious? 'Trust me, you don't want to get to know anything more about me, Carter.'

'Yes I do.'

Why? What had happened to turn him into Mr Sensitive? She wanted him back as Mr Sophisticated—and never-let-a-woman-stick smooth. 'You know, from the moment we met you thought the worst of me,' she provoked. 'I was a thief, I was "pulling favours" to get a good job...'

He actually coloured. 'I didn't really mean—'

'It must be so hard for you to swallow the fact that your thief is the most conservative *man* in the damn building.'

'Yeah, we both know I was wrong. I leapt to a couple of conclusions. You're nothing like what I first thought.'

She turned away from him. 'What if the truth was worse?'

'How worse?' He sounded surprised.

Way, way worse. But she shook her head and dodged it. 'You're as much of a commitment-phobe as I am. Can't we just have some fun, Carter? We've only got a night or two left.'

So many of the women in Carter's life had been total drama queens—living their lives from one big scene to the next, which they maximised as if they were the stars of their own reality TV shows.

Penny wasn't into big scenes at all, even though it appeared her life had had its share of real drama. She'd pared it down, trying to live as simply as possible—at least in terms of her relationships. Getting by on the bare minimum.

But she couldn't deny all of her needs all the time. She needed to be needed—hence her determination to be indispensable in any job she took on. She needed to care for someone—that came out in the way she tended to Mason. She needed physical contact—that came out in the way she sought Carter's body. But he wanted her to want more from him. More than just sex—even though that had been all he'd offered initially, now he wanted her to want it all. He'd always walked from any woman who wanted too much, so wasn't it ironic that, now he wanted to give it all, the woman in question was determined *not* to want it?

Perfectly happy in the past to provide nothing but pleasure, now he wanted to keep her fridge stocked, to make her salmon and salad, to watch her swim every night. He wanted her company, her quiet smiles, her interesting conversation, her compassion. He wanted his kitchen tinged with the scent of cinnamon. He wanted to travel the world with her, explore it the way she did—immersing in a different culture for a while, exploring the arts and politics and being interested. And damn it, there was even that newfound soft secret part of him that wanted to hold her, and to see her holding a tiny, sweet body. The thought of a baby with black-brown eyes and full cream skin made his arms ache.

He wanted everything with her. And he wanted her to have everything. She needed it and he yearned to give it to her—to make her smiles shadow free. To give her some kind of home. He, who'd been happy for so long in his inner-city apartment, was now thinking about a place with a private tennis court and swimming pool and space to play with her.

But he was in trouble. Because although she'd opened her body to him, he had a lot of work ahead of him to get anywhere near her heart.

Carter wasn't used to wanting things he might not be able to achieve. Carter wasn't used to failure. And the threat of failure made Carter angry.

He'd wanted her to tell him about Dan herself but she wasn't going to. The resulting frustration flared out of control. In desperation he wielded a sword, hoping to pierce through her armour to let whatever it was that festered deep inside her free, so she could heal.

He kissed her—hard, passionate and at great length. She wanted it. He could feel her shaking for it. And she thought she'd won—that she'd shut him up. At that moment he pulled back and hit her with it fast. So she'd be unprepared and unable to hide an honest response.

'I know about Dan.'

Her eyes went huge. Shimmering pits of inky blackness. 'What?'

'I know about Dan,' he repeated and then followed up fast. His need to communicate almost making him stumble. 'I know you loved him. I know how much you loved him. I know your grief literally ate you up.'

'What?' Penny couldn't feel her body, and her thoughts were spinning. What had Carter just said?

'I know how hurt you are.'

'You don't know anything.' She walked out of his arms as a ghost walked through walls. No resistance, not feeling anything. She didn't know who he'd been talking to but it was obvious he hadn't got even half the story.

'You can't let losing him stop you from ever loving

anyone again,' Carter said passionately. 'You can't be lonely like this.'

'I'm not lonely.'

'You're crippled with loneliness. You're screaming for affection but you're too scared to admit it.'

She stared at him, utter horror rising in every cell. This couldn't be happening, he just couldn't be going there. He couldn't be asking her about that.

'Please tell me about it,' he asked. 'Let me help you.'

She couldn't bear to see the concern in his eyes. The compassion. The sincerity. He really didn't know anything.

Sick to her stomach, she turned away, pulling the halves of her blouse back together.

'Damn it, don't hide from me.' His volume upped. 'You promised to be honest with me, remember?'

'You really want honesty?' She swung back, stabbing the question.

He paused, his eyes widening in surprise.

She puffed out angrily. He had no idea he'd just taken the scab off the pus-filled hole in her soul. And spilling the poison would spoil their last days together. But there was no avoiding it, he'd pushed over a line she never let anyone past and one look at him told her he wasn't going to let it go.

'It wasn't grief killing my appetite, it was guilt.' The raw, ugly truth choked and burned her throat. 'I didn't love him. That's the whole point.'

Carter froze. Her breathing sped up even more. She hated him for what he was asking her to do. Thinking on this, remembering, speaking of it… It had been so long but it still crucified her heart. She tried to say it simply, quickly. So then she could go. Because then Carter would want her to.

'Dan was my best friend's twin.'

She could see him processing—quickly.

'Isabelle.'

She nodded and pushed on. 'We were neighbours. Born the same year, grew up together. Like triplets, you know? But when we were sixteen, Dan and I...grew close.' She ran her tongue across dry lips. 'It just happened. It was so easy. We were just kids...'

But there was no excusing what she'd done. She closed her eyes; she didn't want to see Carter's reaction. Her breathing quickened more; she couldn't seem to get enough air into her lungs to stop the spinning.

'Everything changed that last year at school. I changed. Isabelle changed.' Penny shook her head, trying to clear it. 'Dan didn't change—at least, not in the same direction.' She sighed. 'We were together a year or so, but I was bored. I had plans and they were different from his.'

Icy sweat slithered across her skin, her blood beat just as cold.

'He didn't want us to break up. He cried. I hadn't seen him cry in years. And do you know what I did?'

Beneath her closed lids, the tears stung. 'I giggled. I actually laughed at him.'

Looking back, it had been the reaction of a silly young girl taken by surprise by his extreme reaction. She hadn't realised he hadn't seen the end of them coming—that she'd shocked him. But she was the one who hadn't seen the most important signs of all—his distance, his depression, his desperation.

She flashed her eyes open and stared hard at Carter,

pushing through the last bit. 'Our orchard ran between our houses and was lined with these big tall trees.'

Her heart thundered as the memory took over her mind completely. 'He was more upset than I realised. The next morning when I got up I looked out the window. And he…and he…'

She couldn't finish. Couldn't express the horror of the shadow in the half-light that she'd seen from her bedroom. She felt the fear as she'd run down the stairs, the damp of the dew on her bare feet as she'd run, slipping, seeing the ladder lying on the grass.

Carter muttered something. She didn't hear what but all of a sudden his arms were around her as her lungs heaved. And this time she heard his horrible realisation.

'You found him.'

Hanging.

Penny raised her hands, trying to hide from the memory. The scream ripped out from the depths of her pain. She twisted, to run, but his arms tightened even more. His whole body pinned her back and pulled her down to the ground.

Her scream became a wail—a long cry of agony that she'd held for so long. The expression of a pain that never seemed to lessen—that just lay buried for days, weeks, months, years until something lifted the veil and let it out.

And now it reverberated around the room—the anguish piercing through walls, smashing through bones. Until Carter absorbed it, pulling her closer still, pressing her face into his chest. His hands smoothing down her hair and over her back as she sobbed.

She hated it. Hated him for making her say it. Hated remembering. Hated the guilt. Hated Dan for doing it.

Hated herself for not stopping him.

And for not being able to stop her meltdown now. She cried and cried and cried while Carter steadily rocked her. She hadn't been held like this in so, so long. Hadn't let anyone—but she couldn't pull away from him now.

She'd broken.

He bent his head, resting it on hers as he kept swaying them both gently even as her shudders began to ease. He said nothing—something she appreciated because there really was nothing to say. It had happened. It was a part of her. Nothing could make it better.

Nothing could make it go away. It would never be okay.

Finally she stilled. She closed her eyes and drew on the last drops of strength that she knew she had—for she was a survivor.

But in order to survive, she had to be alone.

She pushed out of his arms. She didn't want to look at him, her eyes hurt enough already.

'Talk to me,' he said softly.

'Why?' What was the point? She wiped her cheeks with the back of her hand, shaking her head as she did. 'You didn't sign up for this, Carter. You're going away. You don't want baggage and I come with a tonne. A million tonnes.'

Finally she glanced at him. He looked pale. She wasn't surprised. It was a hell of a lot to dump on anyone. And the last thing Carter wanted was complication—he'd made that more than clear right from the start.

And, yeah, he wasn't looking at her any more. All the pretence had gone. All the play had gone. He'd wanted her naked? Well, now she was stripped bare and what was left wasn't pretty.

Anger filled the void that the agony had drained. Why had he forced it? Why pry where he had no right to pry? This was a one-week fling, supposed to be fun, and he'd wrenched open her most private hell.

And for what? Where was the 'fun' to come from this?

'Penny…'

'Don't.' She didn't want his pity. She didn't want him thinking he had to be super-nice to her now because she had problems in her past.

'I want you to talk to me. I want to help you.'

She wasn't a cot-case who needed kid gloves and sympathy. That was second best to what she really wanted.

'No, you don't,' she struck out. 'You think you're so grown-up and mature with your sophisticated little flings. All so charming and satisfying. But you don't want to handle anything really grown up. You don't want emotional responsibility.'

'Penny—'

'And I don't want anything more from you either.' Her fury mounted, and she lied to cover the gaping hole inside. Her biggest lie ever. Desperately she wanted forgiveness and understanding and someone to love her despite all her mistakes.

For Carter to love her.

But he wanted to be her *friend*. And she couldn't accept that because there was that stupid, desperate part of her that wanted to crawl back in his arms and beg him to hold her, to want her, to love her. She couldn't do that to herself. The end hurt enough already and he'd feel awkward enough about easing away from her now. She had to escape to save him from her humiliation. Tears streamed again so she moved fast. Scrabbling to her feet, she literally sprinted.

'Penny!'

She heard a thud and a curse. But she kept running. Running was the only right answer.

For hours she walked the streets, trying to pull herself together.

Putting the memories back into the box was something she was used to. But putting away her feelings for Carter was harder. They were new and fragile and painful. Yeah, she strode out faster, she was as selfish as she'd been as a teen—wanting only what she wanted. Wanting everything for herself.

But she wasn't going to get it.

Determinedly she thought back over what she'd eaten that day. Not enough. She made herself buy a sandwich from a twenty-four-hour garage. Chewed every bite and swallowed even though it clogged her throat. She grabbed a bottle of juice and washed the lumps of bread down. She wasn't going to get sick again. She wasn't going to let heartbreak destroy her body or her mind. She'd get through this—after all, she'd gotten through worse.

She'd stay strong. She'd rebuild her life. She'd done it before and she'd do it again. Only the thought made her aches deepen. Always alone. She was tired of doing it alone. But she always would be alone—because she didn't deserve anything more.

She didn't deserve someone like Carter. Funny, intelligent, gorgeous Carter who could have any woman on a plate and who frankly liked the smorgasbord approach. Her eyes watered and it hurt because they were still sore from her earlier howling. Pathetic. What she needed was to pull herself together and move on. For there was no way she'd stay any longer in Sydney now. Her skin had been burnt from her body—leaving her raw and bloody and too hurt to bear any salt. And, with the memory of a few days of happiness it would hold for ever, Sydney was all salt.

CHAPTER TEN

CARTER was furious. And desperate. Penny had jumped up so fast, and he'd followed only to trip, having totally forgotten that his damn trousers were still round his ankles. In the three seconds it had taken to yank them back up, she'd vanished.

He went to her flat. She wasn't there.

He went to her work. She wasn't there.

He went to her favourite club. She wasn't there.

He went to every open-late café in the neighbourhood, and the neighbourhoods beyond. And then back to the beginning again.

She still wasn't anywhere.

He searched all damn night. But he couldn't find her. Nor could he think of what to say or do when he did. He was beside himself. So upset for her and mad with his stupidity. Hadn't he always said it—the details, it was always in the details.

He hadn't realised the absolute horror of the detail.

Poor Dan. Poor Penny. Poor everyone in their families.

How did anyone get over that? What could he say that could possibly make it better for her? There was nothing. He felt so useless. Right now he *was* useless.

No wonder she'd been worried about how he'd spoken to Aaron-the-flowers-man. No wonder she skated through life with only the occasional fling with a confident player. She was terrified of intimacy. And he didn't blame her.

And she was right, he hadn't signed up for this. He hated this kind of complication, hadn't ever wanted such soul-eating turmoil. He liked fun, uncomplicated. Not needy.

But it was too late. Way, way too late.

He had too much invested already. Like his whole heart.

And despite the way she constantly uprooted her life, she couldn't stop her real nature and needs emerging. She was the one who knew all about the security guard's family, she was the one running round mothering Mason. She couldn't stop herself caring about people. She couldn't stop forming relationships to some degree. But she couldn't accept anywhere near as well as she could give.

Yet surely, surely in her heart she wanted to. That perfect boyfriend she'd described in her emails wasn't the ideal she thought her family would want, it was her own secret ideal.

Yeah, it was there—all in the details. That was her projecting the innermost fantasy that she was too scared to ever try to make real. Well, he could make her laugh. He'd dine and dance with her and take her away on little trips every weekend. He'd be there for her. Always there. Companionship. Commitment. For ever and happy.

Yeah, maybe there wasn't anything he could *say* to make it better. But there was something he could do. He could offer her security. The emotional security and commitment he'd sworn never to offer anyone. For her possible happiness he'd cross all his boundaries. She needed security more than he needed freedom.

Anyway, he wasn't free any more. He was all hers.

He just had to get her to accept it. As he'd got her to accept taking physical pleasure from him, he'd help her accept the love she deserved.

Somehow. He just didn't know how the hell how.

As he drove round and round the streets he rifled through his pockets to find Matt's number. He didn't care about calling New Zealand at such an insane hour. He needed all the details he could get to win this one.

Penny rang Mason's doorbell, so glad he was having another day at home and she didn't have to go into the office. He opened the door and greeted her with a big smile. She tried so hard to return it but knew she failed. Nervously she followed him through to the lounge. But her fast-thumping heart seized when she saw someone was already sitting in there. Someone dishevelled in black jeans and tee with shaggy hair, stubble and hollow, burning eyes.

'Don't mind Carter.' Mason grinned, apparently oblivious to the tortured undercurrents. 'Is that for me?' He nodded at the envelope in her hand.

Penny couldn't take her eyes off Carter, but he had his eyes on the envelope.

She handed it to Mason, amazed she hadn't dropped it. It took only a moment for him to read it. Miserably, guiltily, she waited.

The stark disappointment in Mason's expression was nothing on the barren look of Carter's.

'I'm really sorry, Mason,' she choked out the inadequate apology.

'That's okay, Penny. I'm sure you have your reasons.'

He left the sentence open—not quite a question, but the hint of inquiry was there. She couldn't answer him. She didn't even blush—her blood was frozen.

'Well, you'll stay and have some tea?' Mason asked, now looking concerned.

'I'm sorry,' she said mechanically. 'I really have to go.'

'Right now?' Mason frowned.

'That's okay.' Carter stood, lightly touching Mason's shoulder as he walked past him. 'I'll walk you out, Penny.'

'You don't have to do this, you know,' he launched in as soon as the front door closed behind them. 'I'm leaving later. You can stay and carry on like normal.'

'It's got nothing to do with you,' she lied, devastated to hear he'd made his plans out of there. Even though she knew he would have.

His lips compressed. 'You're happy here, Penny.'

No, she'd been deluding herself. Pretending everything was fine. But he'd come along and ripped away the mirage and shown her just how unfulfilled she really was. It was all a sham.

So she'd go somewhere new and start over. Maybe try to stay there longer, work a little harder on settling. Because now she knew her current way of doing things wasn't really working. It was just a façade.

She knew she'd never forget what had happened between them, but she couldn't stay in Sydney and be faced with a daily reminder of how close she'd been to bliss. 'It's time for me to move on anyway.'

'So you're quitting? You're just going to run away?' Carter's composure started to crack. 'What about Mason? What about the company? You're just going to up and leave him in the lurch?'

'I'm just a temp, Carter.'

'You're not and you know you're not,' he said sharply. 'That old guy in there thinks the world of you. Jed thinks the world of you. All the guys think the world of you. I—' He broke off. 'Damn it, Penny. These people want you in their lives.'

'Give them a week and they'll have moved on.'

'While you'll be stuck in the same hell you've been in the last seven years.' He shook his head. 'You can't let what Dan did ruin the rest of your life.'

She wasn't going to. But she knew what she could and couldn't handle and she couldn't handle the responsibility of close relationships. It scared her too much. And it wasn't just what Dan had done—it was what she'd done.

'It was just as much me, Carter,' she said with painful, angry honesty. 'I was a spoilt, immature bitch who shredded his world. I was horrible to him.'

'He was high, Penny. You know they found drugs in his system. He was struggling with school, with sporting pressure, feeling left behind by your success. He had depression. You didn't know that at the time.'

Oh, he'd got the whole story now. He must have talked to Matt. And even though she knew those things were true, she still felt responsible—certain her actions had been the last straw for Dan's fragile state. 'But I should have known, shouldn't I? If I'd cared. Instead I lost patience. I told him he needed to man up. I was insensitive and selfish.' She admitted it all. 'It was my fault.'

'No.' Carter put heavy hands on her shoulders. 'You didn't kill him. That was a decision he made when he was out of his mind on pot and booze. He was sick.'

'And I should have helped him. Or found someone to help him. I should have told someone about the break-up.'

'There were many factors at play. What happened with you was only one of them.'

If only she'd told someone how badly Dan had reacted. If only she'd told Isabelle that he was really upset and to watch him. But she'd been too selfish to even think of it. She'd gone home feeling free—because he'd become a drain on her. But he'd gone home and decided which way to kill himself.

Even now, her self-centredness horrified her.

'Don't shut everybody out, Penny. Don't let two lives be ruined by one tragic teenage mistake.'

'I'm not shutting everybody out.' She tried to shrug him off. 'I like traveling, Carter. I'm happy.'

'Like hell you are.' His hands tightened.

'I want to go someplace new.' Doggedly she stuck to her line. It was her only option.

He drew breath, seeming to size her up. 'Okay, then I've got an option for you. Move to Melbourne. Move in with me.'

It was good he still had his hands on her—if it weren't for those digging fingertips, she might have fallen over. 'What?'

'Move to Melbourne with me.'

He couldn't possibly be serious. What on earth was he thinking?

'Penny, I've spent the last twelve hours out of my mind with worry for you. I don't want more of that.'

And there was her answer. He wasn't thinking. It was pity and responsibility he was feeling—and exhaustion. Not a real desire to be with her. He didn't love her. She couldn't possibly believe he did.

'I didn't mean to make you worry,' she said quietly. It was the last thing she'd wanted to do to him. That was the problem with her family too. She'd made them worry so much. That was why she tried to email home the breezy-life-is-easy vibe.

Only clearly she'd failed at that because Carter had been talking to Matt. And they'd conspired together to sort her out somehow. But she wasn't going to let compassion trick Carter into thinking he wanted to be with her. That was worse than anything his ex had deliberately tried to manipulate.

'I don't need you to rescue me, Carter,' she said softly.

'That's not what I'm trying to do.'

'Isn't it?'

'I want us to be together.'

'Well—' she took a deep breath '—I don't.'

'I know you're lying.' He leaned close. 'You want me to prove it to you?'

She stepped back. No, she did not want that. She couldn't bear it if he kissed her right now. She'd be ripped apart.

His smile flattened. 'What are you going to do, put us all on your occasional email list and send details of your fictional life?' His anger suddenly blew. 'The minute you feel yourself putting down roots, you wrench yourself away again. It's emotional suicide.'

She struck out—shoving him hard.

How dared he? How *dared* he say that to her?

'It *is*, Penny.' He squared up to her again. 'You're too scared to live a whole life.'

Her only defence was offence. 'And you're living a whole one?'

'I want to. I want you.'

'No, you don't.' He felt some stupid honourable responsibility.

'So you just quit? Is that the lesson you learned from Dan—to give up?'

'Don't.' She took another step back from him. 'Just don't. You can't ever understand what it was like.'

'Maybe not, but I can try—I would if you'd let me. Damn it, Penny, I don't want to just have fun any more. I want to be happy. I want you to be happy. I want everything. And I want it with you.' His words tumbled. 'We could do so much together. We could do great things.'

The urge to ask was irresistible. 'Like what?'

'Like have a family.'

She caught her breath in a quick gasp, blinking rapidly as she shook her head. But he knew, didn't he? He'd seen her flash of longing.

His fleeting smile twisted. 'You just told me you were selfish back then. But don't you think you're being selfish now? Denying not just yourself, but me too?'

'The last thing I need is more guilt, Carter.'

'No, I'm strong, Penny,' he answered roughly. 'You can throw your worst at me and I'll survive. You'll survive too. I know you've found yourself a way to survive. But you're too afraid to live.'

Her eyes burned, her throat burned, her heart burned.

'Are you brave enough to fight for what you really want?' Somehow he'd got right back in front of her, whispering, tempting. So beautiful that she couldn't do anything but stare.

And then her heart tore.

For there was no point to this—what she wanted she didn't deserve. And the person she wanted deserved so much more than what she could give him.

'I don't want to hurt anyone the way I hurt him,' she breathed.

'No, *you* don't want to be hurt. And that's okay. I won't hurt you.' His eyes shone that brilliant green-blue—clearer than a mountain stream. 'I'm offering everything I have. Everything I never wanted to give is yours—you just have to take it.'

'I can't.'

'Why not?'

Because she'd never believe that he really meant this. And he was wrong about how strong she was. She wouldn't survive it when he realised the huge mistake he'd made.

'I just can't.'

Carter stood on the path and watched her walk further and further away. Slowly ripping his heart out with every step. He hadn't meant to lay it all out like that—not when he was angry and she was angry. He knew she'd need time. But she'd blindsided him with the speed of her resignation and intention to run. And her rejection. It hurt. So he'd thrown all his chips down, gambled everything—too much, too soon. And he'd blown it.

CHAPTER ELEVEN

PICK a destination. Any destination. Anywhere had to be better than here.

Penny stared at the departures board but the only place her eyes seemed willing to see was Melbourne.

Melbourne, Melbourne, Melbourne.

She could go to Perth—lots of sun in Perth. But there was art and champion sport in Melbourne. How about Darwin or Alice Springs—maybe a punishing climate was what she deserved. But Melbourne had a superb café culture and fabulous shopping.

She slumped into the nearest seat.

Carter would be flying out there soon. If he hadn't already.

Yeah, that was the draw. Melbourne had Carter.

She really ought to go to the international terminal and go halfway round the globe. Instead she sat in the chair, tears falling. Not sobbing, just steady tears that leaked from her eyes and dribbled down her cheeks and onto her top. People were looking sideways but she didn't care. It was normal for people to cry at airports. Okay, so maybe it wasn't quite so normal to sit for over an hour staring at the destination board with only a small suitcase and not having bought a ticket yet. Not having even chosen where to go, let alone what to do once she got there.

She regretted the decision. But it was the only decision she'd been able to make and it had hurt. So much. There was no going back. She could never go back. She could never have what her heart wanted the most.

But it whispered. It constantly whispered—beating hope.

He'd said she was strong. She wasn't at all. He'd been more right when he'd said she was afraid. That was totally true. She hadn't laid herself on the line. And he had. What if he'd really meant it? Could she honestly live the rest of her life always wondering what if? And even if he hadn't meant it, even if he might change his mind, wasn't it time for her to be honest about her own emotions anyway?

He deserved her honesty. It was the one thing he'd asked from her but she'd lied to him at the most crucial moment and that was so unfair. Even to the last she'd held back. He'd been right. She did torpedo her relationships when people got too close. She was a huge coward.

No more. Even if nothing else happened, she needed to prove to herself that she could be more than that. She needed to express her feelings openly. It was beyond time she faced up to them. To her family. To everything.

Carter had shown her how beautifully her body could work if she let go, maybe his other gift was to help her grow true courage.

She went up to the counter. It took less than three minutes to purchase a ticket. The departure lounge wasn't far. She sat and waited for the boarding call. Beyond that she couldn't think.

Finally the call was made. She reached down to pick

up her pack, about to stand to join the queuing passengers. But right by her pack was a pair of big black boots, topped by black jeans. Someone was standing in front of her.

She looked up at the tall figure with the hair so tousled it stood on end, the creased tee and jeans, the unnaturally bright blue-green eyes.

'I've been sitting in that café over there,' he said. 'Watching, waiting, wanting to know what you were going to do. Where you were going to go. I've had four long blacks. It's been almost two hours.' He sat in the seat next to hers. 'So, where are you going?'

Surely he knew already—they'd just announced the flight. Emotion swelled inside her, becoming so huge she had to let it out. It was bigger than her, and she was only hurting herself more by trying to deny or control it or hide it. She held up the boarding pass for him to read: *Melbourne*.

As he stared at the card the colour washed out of his face, leaving him as pale as he'd been the night before. Then he looked at her again, she stared back. Her eyes filled with tears but she couldn't blink, couldn't break the contact with him. Wordlessly wanting him to know, to believe beyond any doubt just how much he meant to her.

Abruptly he turned, facing the window. The plane waited out on the runway, the luggage carts were driven warp speed by the baggage handlers. And with her fingers she squeezed her ragged tissue into a tighter and tighter ball.

She heard him clear his throat but still he said nothing. Her doubts returned—had she just freaked him out? Was he regretting what he'd said earlier already?

But then he held out his hand. The simple gesture seemed to offer so much. She drew a sharp, shuddering breath and put her hand on his.

He guided her to stand beside him. With his other hand he scooped up the handle of her case, wheeling it behind them—away from the flight queue.

She couldn't really see where they were going, the tears still fell too fast. And she kept her head down, unsure if she could believe this was actually happening or if she'd gone delusional.

'The great thing about airports is that they have hotels very close by.' He sounded raspy. He matched his pace to hers—slow—but kept them moving steadily. 'You need a shower and a rest, Penny. You look beat. And I need...' He stopped and closed his eyes for a moment. Then he took a deep breath and began walking again. 'We'll fly tomorrow.'

They went out of the doors and straight into a taxi.

'How did you find me?' she asked once Carter had instructed the driver.

'Been stalking you all day.' His hand tightened.

'Why did you wait so long?'

His expression twisted. 'I thought you were going to go somewhere else. I sat there and waited. It was torture. Every minute I expected you to just get up and go to the counter and buy a ticket who knew where. But then you did and you went to that departure lounge and I had to see if you were really going to do it.'

'It was the only place I could go.'

He was silent a long moment. 'Why did it take you so long to realise?'

'Because I was scared.'

'Of what?'

'My feelings for you.' Her whisper could hardly be heard. 'Your feelings for me.'

He turned his head sharply, but the taxi stopped, interrupting them. But it took only a few minutes to book into the hotel, another couple to ride the lift and then be in privacy.

She walked into the middle of the room—needing to say her piece before passion overtook her mind. 'I don't want you to feel like you have to rescue me, Carter. I don't want your pity.'

'I have no intention of rescuing you. I want to rescue myself.'

That startled her. 'From what?'

'From a life of meaningless flings.' He shrugged and looked sheepish. 'In fact there wouldn't be any more flings anyway. I don't want to sleep with another woman ever. Only you. So, you see, you have to rescue me from a life of celibacy and terminal boredom.'

'Carter—'

'I'm not the person I was a couple of weeks ago,' he said quickly. 'I believe in you like I've never believed in another woman. I trust you like I've never trusted another woman. You make me want to love and be with just one woman.'

She swallowed. Yeah, she still couldn't quite believe that. 'I'm hardly exciting. I'm not flashy or amazingly talented or anything. I'm just a temp PA.'

He walked nearer. 'You want to know what you are, Penny?' He reached up to tuck her hair behind her ear. 'You're warm, you're funny. You're competitive, you definitely have your ball-breaker moments. Sometimes you're misguided but you're passionate in everything you do. You have such heart. You can't hide it. And I want it.'

But it was still a very scared heart.

'You'll like Melbourne,' he said. 'We can find a house. My apartment is nice but we need more space and our own private pool and a deck big enough to dance on so you can have raves at home.' He winked. 'It takes a couple of weeks to organise the licence but we'll get married as soon as it's possible.'

She shook her head, had to interrupt the fantasy at that point. 'Carter, that's crazy talk. We've only known each other a week.'

'Nearly two,' he corrected.

'Yeah, and I've been on my best behaviour.'

Laughter burst from him—just a brief shout. She gave his shoulder a little push, but inside the fear was resurging. This was happening too fast—he'd changed his mind too fast; he might change it back again just as quick.

'I'm serious. You can't go making a decision like this so quickly. I'm a cow. I get moody. I get itchy feet.'

'Okay.' He gripped her just above the elbows and pulled her close. 'Here's the deal. You move to Melbourne and move in with me. I'm making my claim public and I'm proud to. Give us six months to settle, and then I'm asking you again. I guarantee we'll be even happier by then. There'll be no answer but yes.'

'Six months is still too soon.' It was still lust-fuelled infatuation territory—for him anyway. For her, well, her heart had long been lost to him already.

'It isn't. You know it isn't. You can trust me. There's nothing about you that's going to put me off. I already know you're not perfect, Penny. No one is. But we can both be better people together.'

She couldn't move, too scared to blink in case she was dreaming this. Was she really this close to having everything? Still the shadows in her heart made her doubt.

'Six months to the day, sweetheart,' he said firmly. 'And I'll tell you what else.' His hands firmed up too. 'I'm taking you home. You take my hand and we go to your parents' anniversary party Matt told me about. And you show me that tree. We'll face it together, and maybe we'll plant something under it. A bulb or something so every spring a new flower will grow and then it'll die and then another will grow. You like to leave the flowers to grow, right? But we'll grow too—we'll get on with life together. And maybe in a year or two we'll grow a family together.'

Penny pressed her curled hands to her chest, unable to say anything, unable to blink the searing tears away.

'I know you're scared.' He gently cupped her face. 'But I'll be with you and I won't let you down.'

She pressed her cheek into his palm. 'I don't want to let you down either.'

'You won't. Give us the time. You know this is right. You know how happy we're going to be. We already are. You just have to let it happen.'

'You have the details all worked out.'

'I do.' His gaze dropped for a moment. 'You once promised me honesty. Will you give me it now?'

'Yes.' That was the least she could give him.

He paused, seeming to consider his words. 'Do you really…want me?'

Her eyeballs ached, her temples, her throat and all the way down her middle right to her toes—every cell in her system screamed its agony. 'Oh, yes,' she cried. 'It hurts so much.'

'It doesn't have to hurt, sweetheart.' His arms crushed her tight. 'It doesn't have to.'

He lifted his head so he held her gaze, seeing right into her. And she should have been afraid. For a second the panic swept up in a wave inside her because he saw it all. How deep her longing went. But then he kissed her.

And then, for the first time, his patience left him.

'I need to be with you,' he groaned. 'I need to feel you.'

Now she saw his vulnerability. Saw just how much her leaving would have hurt him. How much he'd been hiding from her—or more that she'd been too blinded by fear to be able to see. How much he wanted her, and wanted to care for her.

He whipped off his top, undid hers too. His hands shook and fumbled to unzip her skirt and slide it off. His breathing roughened, his hands roughened.

So she helped and soon she was naked and he was naked and warming her. He didn't kiss her all over, didn't tease or torment her with his fingers or tongue. He just held her close and kissed her as if there was nothing else on earth he'd ever want to do, as if he needed her more than anything.

She loved the weight of him on her. The way he held her hair hard so he could kiss her. The way he ground his body and soul into her. He moved—all power and passion and pure frantic force. He held—truly, tenderly, tightly held her as he poured his want and need and love as deeply into her as he could. And she clung, feeling the sublime beauty between them, so awed that they could make such magic together. And then there was no room for thought. She was reduced to absolute essence—pure emotion.

'I'm sorry,' he panted. 'I just couldn't hold back.'

She turned towards him and smiled.

He lifted his head slightly from the pillow, his eyebrows shooting up. 'No way.'

She nodded.

'You're not just saying that?'

'I'll never fake it with you. Never have. Never will.' She gazed at him. 'I loved it. I loved feeling how desperate you were to touch me.'

'I've been desperate to touch you since the minute we met.' It wasn't a teasing comment, but honest vulnerability.

She snuggled closer, so content she thought she might burst. And the fantasy he'd painted for her rose in her head.

'You really want children?' she wondered aloud—her heart still stuttered over that step too far into the realm of paradise.

'Can't have Nick acting all spoilt like he's an only child. He needs a nephew or niece to give him a run for it,' he joked. But the next second he went totally sober again. 'I never thought I wanted them. Or marriage. You know that. But it took meeting the one woman who's so right for me to make me realise just how much I do want those things. The problem before was that I hadn't met you. Now I have. So now I know.'

The most incredible feeling of peace descended on Penny—as if he'd soothed every inch of her, inside and out. With utter serenity and certainty, her faith blossomed in the strong man beside her. In herself. In what they already shared and could yet share if she let them.

She shifted position, curling even closer and resting her head on his chest.

'Your heart is beating so fast.' She swept her hand across his skin, feeling the strong thudding beneath. 'Must be all that coffee.'

Carter let out a helpless grunt of laughter. 'No. It's you. All you.'

He slid his hand down her arm, down the slim wrist, until his palm pressed over hers. He bent his fingers and felt her mirror the action, locking their hands together.

'I love you,' she finally whispered. 'I love you so much. I want to live with you at my side.'

'Then that's where I'll be.' Carter trembled. Having never before in his life trembled, he trembled now as he felt her absolute acceptance of him. And of every ounce of love he had to offer.

Their future had just been born.

CHAPTER TWELVE

Five and a half months later.

PENNY sat glued to her laptop, trying to fritter away the last hour before Carter got home. Thank heavens that in New Zealand Matt was still at work and she could instant message him.

Have you asked that cute bookstore girl out for a date yet?

Working up the courage. Concentrate on your own love life.

Working up the courage here too.

Why are you scared? He'll love it. He loves you. He put up with Mum and Dad fawning for an entire week for you. Case proven.

Still scared. OK, excited too. Very excited.

Bordering on TMI.

Ha-ha. Wish it was over already.

'Where are you?'

Penny jumped as Carter called out downstairs. She hadn't even heard the door. A stupidly happy giggle bubbled out, even though her heart started thudding so fast it threatened to dance right out of her chest.

Have to go. He's here.

She slammed her laptop shut and raced down the stairs to meet her so very real man. Nervous as she was, she couldn't stop her smiles, lifting her face to kiss him. He was earlier than she'd asked him to be. But then he always gave her more than she asked for. And she loved him for that.

'So why do you need me home from work so early?'

'An adventure,' she said, her mouth cabin-bread dry. 'I'm driving,' she said. 'You just sit back and enjoy the ride.'

He followed her out to his car. 'A mystery tour?'

'Yes.' She bit her lip but still couldn't stop smiling. It was that or cry with the nerves.

He'd been right, of course, that day in the airport hotel. Everything had got better. They'd visited her parents, she'd gotten to know his dad and his wife and little Nick. They saw Mason regularly and his company had weathered the skimming scandal no problem. Even the sex between them continued to blossom—she'd never have thought that could possibly improve. But it had. She'd fallen in love with Melbourne too. She temped—short-term contracts—refusing to work for Carter, claiming she needed to maintain an element of independence. Something she knew he wasn't entirely happy about. But he had absolutely no cause to worry.

She, on the other hand, was still nervous.

She drove the route she'd been along a million times already. The last fifty times she'd rehearsed this moment in her head. But the reality wasn't anything like she'd imagined. Every cell was so aware and on edge it was as if she had acute vision and hearing and a heart still beating way too fast.

But in a good way. She wanted it to be so good.

It was the very end of winter, so the garden was at its most dormant phase. But still so very beautiful—private, tranquil and spacious. She walked slightly ahead of him, hoping he didn't mind the dropping temperature of the late afternoon. She showed him the lawn, pointed out the pathways and the water features of the by-appointment-only private grounds that had been built by an older couple—wonderfully mad visionaries whom Penny had gotten to know and adore.

'In six months it'll be summer and there'll be so much colour.' She gestured wide around her. 'Flowers everywhere.' She turned back to face him. 'I won't need a bouquet because we'll be in the midst of one.'

'A bouquet?' A half-step behind, he didn't take his eyes off her.

'Yes…' She swallowed. 'I wanted to know if…' She took a breath. 'Will you marry me? Here? Then?'

He didn't move.

Nor did she.

It was one of those moments that took for ever but where the anticipation was a painful, heart-stopping pleasure. A moment she'd treasure the rest of her life. Because as she watched, the smile stole into his blue and green and gold eyes. It spread to his mouth. And his whole face filled with that rakish, irresistible charm.

'Yes.'

She simply fell into his wide open arms, struggled to get her own around him so she could hold on tighter than ever, kissing him with every particle of passion she had.

Eons later, she managed another breathless question. 'You don't mind I beat you to it?'

'I like it most when you beat me to it.'

She giggled and pressed her hot face into his neck as she whispered, 'I wanted to ask you. I wanted to offer you everything I have.'

Because he'd already given his all to her and she knew it and she wanted to be an equal match for him.

He tugged her hair so she looked back up at him.

'I'm honoured you asked,' he said, intensely sincere. 'I know what you're saying.'

That she truly believed in him, in them and finally in herself.

'I want you to understand how happy I am.' She smiled softly through a trickling tear.

'I do.' He smiled back. 'And nothing would make me happier than to be your husband. We're a really good team, Penny.'

Her smile spread. 'You do realise this means more time with my parents.'

'More time with my step-mother,' he countered.

'You know she's lovely.'

'Just as you know your parents are lovely. And so is Matt.'

She nodded vigorously and they both laughed.

The difference in her life was so dramatic—full of family, full of fun—real, every day and every night joy. It was because of her anchor—the strongest, most loving man. And the most shameless.

Because now he swept her back into his arms and took control of the situation. 'I'm so glad we've got you over your dislike of public displays.'

But there was no one around to watch him pick her up and carry her out of the chill wind, into the glass building that housed the exotic plants in the cold season. And there, under the bowers of some giant green monstrosity of a plant, they made sweet, perfect, sizzling love.

Coming Next Month

from **Harlequin Presents®**. Available July 26, 2011.

#3005 THE MARRIAGE BETRAYAL
Lynne Graham
The Volakis Vow

#3006 THE DISGRACED PLAYBOY
Caitlin Crews
The Notorious Wolfes

#3007 A DARK SICILIAN SECRET
Jane Porter

#3008 THE MATCHMAKER BRIDE
Kate Hewitt
The Powerful and the Pure

#3009 THE UNTAMED ARGENTINEAN
Susan Stephens

#3010 PRINCE OF SCANDAL
Annie West

Coming Next Month

from **Harlequin Presents® EXTRA**. Available August 9, 2011.

#161 REPUTATION IN TATTERS
Maggie Cox
Rescued by the Rich Man

#162 THE IMPOVERISHED PRINCESS
Robyn Donald
Rescued by the Rich Man

#163 THE MAN SHE LOVES TO HATE
Kelly Hunter
Dirty Filthy Money

#164 THE PRIVILEGED AND THE DAMNED
Kimberly Lang
Dirty Filthy Money

Visit www.HarlequinInsideRomance.com
for more information on upcoming titles!

REQUEST YOUR FREE BOOKS!

◆Harlequin *Presents*

PASSION GUARANTEED SEDUCTION

2 FREE NOVELS PLUS
2 FREE GIFTS!

YES! Please send me 2 FREE Harlequin Presents® novels and my 2 FREE gifts (gifts are worth about $10). After receiving them, if I don't wish to receive any more books, I can return the shipping statement marked "cancel." If I don't cancel, I will receive 6 brand-new novels every month and be billed just $4.05 per book in the U.S. or $4.74 per book in Canada. That's a saving of at least 15% off the cover price! It's quite a bargain! Shipping and handling is just 50¢ per book in the U.S. and 75¢ per book in Canada.* I understand that accepting the 2 free books and gifts places me under no obligation to buy anything. I can always return a shipment and cancel at any time. Even if I never buy another book, the two free books and gifts are mine to keep forever.

106/306 HDN FC55

Name	(PLEASE PRINT)	

Address		Apt. #

City	State/Prov.	Zip/Postal Code

Signature (if under 18, a parent or guardian must sign)

Mail to the Reader Service:
IN U.S.A.: P.O. Box 1867, Buffalo, NY 14240-1867
IN CANADA: P.O. Box 609, Fort Erie, Ontario L2A 5X3

Not valid for current subscribers to Harlequin Presents books.

**Are you a current subscriber to Harlequin Presents books
and want to receive the larger-print edition?
Call 1-800-873-8635 or visit www.ReaderService.com.**

* Terms and prices subject to change without notice. Prices do not include applicable taxes. Sales tax applicable in N.Y. Canadian residents will be charged applicable taxes. Offer not valid in Quebec. This offer is limited to one order per household. All orders subject to credit approval. Credit or debit balances in a customer's account(s) may be offset by any other outstanding balance owed by or to the customer. Please allow 4 to 6 weeks for delivery. Offer available while quantities last.

Your Privacy—The Reader Service is committed to protecting your privacy. Our Privacy Policy is available online at www.ReaderService.com or upon request from the Reader Service.

We make a portion of our mailing list available to reputable third parties that offer products we believe may interest you. If you prefer that we not exchange your name with third parties, or if you wish to clarify or modify your communication preferences, please visit us at www.ReaderService.com/consumerschoice or write to us at Reader Service Preference Service, P.O. Box 9062, Buffalo, NY 14269. Include your complete name and address.

HPI1

Once bitten, twice shy. That's Gabby Wade's motto—
especially when it comes to Adamson men.
And the moment she meets Jon Adamson her theory
is confirmed. But with each encounter a little something
sparks between them, making her wonder if she's been
too hasty to dismiss this one!

Enjoy this sneak peek from ONE GOOD REASON
by Sarah Mayberry, available August 2011
from Harlequin® Superromance®.

Gabby Wade's heartbeat thumped in her ears as she marched to her office. She wanted to pretend it was because of her brisk pace returning from the file room, but she wasn't that good a liar.

Her heart was beating like a tom-tom because Jon Adamson had touched her. In a very male, very possessive way. She could still feel the heat of his big hand burning through the seat of her khakis as he'd steadied her on the ladder.

It had taken every ounce of self-control to tell him to unhand her. What she'd really wanted was to grab him by his shirt and, well, explore all those urges his touch had instantly brought to life.

While she might not like him, she was wise enough to understand that it wasn't always about liking the other person. Sometimes it was about pure animal attraction.

Refusing to think about it, she turned to work. When she'd typed in the wrong figures three times, Gabby admitted she was too tired and too distracted. Time to call it a day.

As she was leaving, she spied Jon at his workbench in the shop. His head was propped on his hand as he studied blueprints. It wasn't until she got closer that she saw his eyes were shut.

He looked oddly boyish. There was something innocent and unguarded in his expression. She felt a weakening in her resistance to him.

"Jon." She put her hand on his shoulder, intending to shake him awake. Instead, it rested there like a caress.

His eyes snapped open.

"You were asleep."

"No, I was, uh, visualizing something on this design." He gestured to the blueprint in front of him then rubbed his eyes.

That gesture dealt a bigger blow to her resistance. She realized it wasn't only animal attraction pulling them together. She took a step backward as if to get away from the knowledge.

She cleared her throat. "I'm heading off now."

He gave her a smile, and she could see his exhaustion.

"Yeah, I should, too." He stood and stretched. The hem of his T-shirt rose as he arched his back and she caught a flash of hard male belly. She looked away, but it was too late. Her mind had committed the image to permanent memory.

And suddenly she knew, for good or bad, she'd never look at Jon the same way again.

Find out what happens next in ONE GOOD REASON, available August 2011 from Harlequin® Superromance®!

Celebrating

Blaze **10** years of

red-hot reads

Featuring a special August author lineup of
six fan-favorite authors who have written
for Blaze™ from the beginning!

The Original Sexy Six:

Vicki Lewis Thompson

Tori Carrington

Kimberly Raye

Debbi Rawlins

Julie Leto

Jo Leigh

Pick up all six Blaze™
Special Collectors' Edition titles!

August 2011

USA TODAY *bestselling author*

Lynne Graham

introduces her new Epic Duet

THE VOLAKIS VOW
A marriage made of secrets…

Tally Spencer, an ordinary girl with no experience of
relationships… Sander Volakis, an impossibly rich and
handsome Greek entrepreneur. Sander is expecting to
love her and leave her, but for Tally this is love at first
sight. Little does he know that Tally is expecting his
baby…and blackmailing him to marry her!

PART ONE:
THE MARRIAGE BETRAYAL
Available August 2011

PART TWO:
BRIDE FOR REAL
Available September 2011

Available only from Harlequin Presents®.

www.Harlequin.com

HP13005